ALL OF THE ABOVE

A NOVEL BY SHELLEY PEARSALL

Illustrations by Javaka Steptoe

LITTLE, BROWN AND COMPANY
New York Boston

Copyright © 2006 by Shelley Pearsall
Author's Note copyright © 2017 by Shelley Pearsall
Illustrations copyright © 2006 by Javaka Steptoe

Cover art copyright © 2017 by Erwin Madrid. Cover design by Marcie Lawrence
Cover copyright © 2017 by Hachette Book Group, Inc.

Little, Brown and Company

Hachette Book Group
1290 Avenue of the Americas, New York, NY 10104
Visit us at lb-kids.com

Little, Brown and Company is a division of Hachette Book Group, Inc. The Little, Brown name and logo are trademarks of Hachette Book Group, Inc.

The publisher is not responsible for websites (or their content) that are not owned by the publisher.

First Paperback Edition: January 2008
First published in hardcover in 2006 by Little, Brown and Company

Library of Congress Cataloging-in-Publication Data

Pearsall, Shelley.
All of the above / by Shelley Pearsall. — 1st ed.
    p. cm.
Summary: Four urban middle school students, their teacher, and other community members relate how a school project to build the world's largest tetrahedron affects the lives of everyone involved.
ISBN-13: 978-0-316-11524-7 (hc)
ISBN-13: 978-0-316-11526-1 (pb)
[1. Interpersonal relations — Fiction. 2. Self-confidence — Fiction. 3. Family problems — Fiction. 4. City and town life — Fiction. 5. Geometry — Fiction. 6. Schools — Fiction.] I. Title.
PZ7.P3166All 2006
[Fic] — dc22   2005033109

20 19 18 17

LSC-C

Printed in the United States of America

The text was set in ITC Korrina, and the display type is Campaign.

for the 2002 tetrahedron team members
and their teachers

*I*f you follow Washington Boulevard past the smoky good smells of Willy Q's Barbecue, past the Style R Us hair salon, where they do nails like nobody's business, past the eye-popping red doors of the Sanctuary Baptist Church, you'll finally come to a dead end.

That's where our school sits. Right at the dead end of Washington Boulevard. We know there's a lot of people out there who think our school is a dead end. And that all the kids inside it are dead ends, too.

They drive past our school, roll up their car windows, and lock their doors. Let's get out of this bad neighborhood, they say. Fast.

But they've got it all wrong. Because inside our crumbling, peeling-paint, broken-window school, we are gonna build something big. Something that will make all of them sit up and take notice, even the people with their big, fancy cars and rolled-up windows. Something that hasn't been built in the history of the world. By anybody.

JUST YOU WAIT AND SEE. . . .

MR. COLLINS

Before this story begins, there are a few facts you should know. This is not for a quiz, but if it was, I would tell you to write the following facts *neatly* in your math notebook:

1. Tetrahedrons are geometric solids with four faces. All four faces are equilateral triangles.

2. Small tetrahedrons can be joined together to make larger ones.

3. The largest tetrahedron ever constructed was approximately seven feet tall, and it was made of 4,096 smaller tetrahedrons.

4. It was built by students at a private school in California. They had plenty of time and money.

5. I teach at a city school in Cleveland, Ohio, where I have been a middle school math teacher for the past twenty years.

6. We don't have much time or money.

7. The idea for the tetrahedron project began with one of my worst classes in twenty years of teaching.

8. It happened on a Friday.

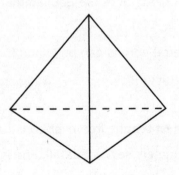

JAMES HARRIS III

I don't listen to nothing in Collins' math class. Only thing I listen for is the bell. That bell at the end of class is just about the sweetest sound in the world. The whole class, I sit there waiting on that bell and watching the hands of the clock jump from one little black mark to the next. You ever notice how school clocks do that? How they don't move like other clocks do; they jump ahead like bugs?

I even saw one move backward once. I swear the hands went five minutes back right before lunch. I told the teacher that the clock was cheating us out of recess and got a detention just for saying that.

Mr. Collins teaches seventh grade math and I'm telling you, straight up, he's one of the worst teachers you can get at Washington Middle School. My older brother, DJ, had him for math two years ago. He told me Collins would do nothing but talk and write on the board for the whole period, and the hardest part of his class was not falling asleep. And forget his tests; don't even bother to try.

Every Friday, me and Terrell and three of the other guys who can keep their big mouths shut take bets on which tie Collins will have on when he walks in. He's been wearing the same ones for forever. DJ's class did the same thing. Everybody put in a quarter and whoever guessed right on the day they were betting got all the money.

It gonna be pea green, puke orange, red stripe, yellow diamond, or dirt brown, today, huh?

I've won three bucks so far this year, and it's only September.

But then one Friday, Collins did something crazy. Like cracked. I was sitting there in class that afternoon staring at the jumping clock like usual, and Collins' voice was going on and on about how important geometry was. Yeah, right. His voice was talking to itself, while his hand drew on the board.

This is a cylinder, class. This is a cube.

Nobody was paying attention to a word he was saying.

This is a cold Pepsi can, my mind said. This is a box with a big, juicy Big Mac inside. No mustard. Extra ketchup.

And then Collins suddenly stops his hand in midair, whips around, and stares at us. "Is anybody listening to me?" He waves his arms and yells. You know, it was almost funny. You could see the little veins in his forehead popping out and his neck starting to turn beet red.

All week he'd been giving us this same line. How nobody in our class was listening to him. What's there to listen to? That's what I kept wanting to ask. Only four people turned in their homework on Tuesday and almost everybody failed his quiz on Wednesday, and you shoulda seen him losing it about that —

But this time he completely flips out. He throws his piece of yellow chalk onto the stack of papers sitting on his desk, goes over to the side of the room, and stands there staring out the windows with his arms crossed. While he's doing that, the piece of chalk rolls off the papers, hits the floor, and shatters into a thousand little pieces. That makes everybody crack up. But Collins, he doesn't even turn around to look. He just keeps standing there at the window, not saying a word.

I swear he doesn't move for about a half hour. You shoulda seen the looks the whole class was giving behind Collins' back while he stood there. Everybody rolling their eyes at each other and pretending to cough and shaking their heads. Like nobody knows what to think.

When Collins finally does turn around, he's got his serious face on. You know the one I'm talking about. Like we are about to get another big long lecture. Maybe because me and Terrell are in the row right next to where he's standing, Collins starts in on us first. I slouch down in my chair, figuring he'll get a clue and move somewhere else. But he doesn't.

"James," he says, "what would make you care about being here?"

"Where?" I ask, trying to give the least answer I can.

"Right here. Math class, room 307, Washington Middle School, Cleveland, Ohio." Collins motions toward the windows. "What would make you want to be right here, in room 307, James?"

"Nothing. I hate math," I say to Collins, and the whole class starts laughing.

"I'm sorry to hear that," the teacher answers in a strange voice once the class gets quiet again. He moves on to Terrell next. "You, Terrell? What about you?"

Behind me, Terrell's answer is too low to hear. I mean I hear it because that's the way me and Terrell talk all the time in class, but Collins doesn't. He comes walking closer to him. "I didn't hear exactly what you answered," he warns.

"Maybe some kinda contest," Terrell mumbles.

I swear under my breath. *You tell him about the ties and you're a dead man, Terrell.* DJ and the others would never let me forget it if Collins found out. I could hear my brother already — "Figures you'd be the fools who'd go and give away the whole thing. Been doing this for years and your class had to be the one that snitched."

"A contest . . ." Collins repeats Terrell's words like he always does with whatever you answer. "What kind of contest?"

I can hear Terrell shifting around in his seat behind me. "Just a contest," he mumbles again, "or
something like that."

For about a minute, the teacher stands there staring into space like he's thinking about Terrell's answer or waiting to hear something more. Then he
goes back up to the chalkboard, erases the whole
thing, and starts drawing these big crazy lines. The
chalk goes *screak, screak, screak,* like fingernails
scraping, he draws so hard. He slashes one diagonal
chalk line from the top of the board to the bottom,
then a straight line top to bottom, then another diagonal one, then a few more at the bottom until there is
something that looks like a big pyramid on the board.

"Anybody know what this is?" he says loudly, rap-
ping his knuckles on the board.

Nobody says a word. I think everybody believes
Collins has lost his mind.

"T-E-T-R-A-H-E-D-R-O-N" the teacher writes in
big crooked letters across the whole board. Then, he
whips around and shouts, "WHY AREN'T ANY OF
YOU WRITING THIS DOWN?"

I yank Terrell's pencil out of his hand and tell him

he had better keep his fat mouth shut for the rest of class. On the inside cover of one of my notebooks, I copy the word from the board. TETRA HEED RON. That's what I put down.

While Collins is writing the definition, I draw a guy standing on a tall, pointy mountain with the words "Help me, help me! I'm Tetra Heed Ron" coming out of the guy's mouth. That cracks me up. I turn around to show it to Terrell and a shadow falls across my desk.

"I'll take that notebook," Collins says. The little metal spirals make a zipping sound as he pulls it right out of my hand and tosses it onto his desk. *Man*, another detention. I slam my chair back so hard it hits Terrell's desk behind me.

"Starting on Monday, here's the contest we are going to have," Collins says to the class.

I don't even listen. Who cares about some dumb math contest?

"We are going to have a contest to build one of these." Collins smacks his palm on the chalkboard pyramid and chalk dust flies up in the air. "A tetrahedron. Nobody has ever made one larger than six levels before. That's the record. So, our school is going to build a bigger one." Collins looks around the classroom like he is expecting us to be excited about his crazy idea. "So what do you think? Who wants to give this a try?"

Not one single person raises their hand, because what kind of contest is that? Building a pyramid? How's that gonna make math class any better? But the teacher keeps going on and on. Telling us how some school in California holds the world record. How their six-level one had 4,096 pieces. How our school could get into the *Guinness Book of World Records* if we do this. How we could be on the news across the country.

Yeah, right. I just keep my eyes on the jumping clock.

"How about it, Terrell? It was your idea to have a contest," Collins says, walking around trying to convince people. "Donte — how about you? Or Sharice? Rhondell?"

The teacher looks over at me again. "James — you have art talent. You could do this. Don't you want to be in the *Guinness Book of World Records* for something? Don't you want to see your name right there on its own page" — he draws a page in the air with his hands — "James Harris III?"

No. *Wish you would just get away from me, fool, that's what I wish.*

Sharice, who's always kissing up to the teachers, says maybe. And Rhondell Jeffries, who's got brains but is nothing to look at, says she'll think about it, too. Nobody else agrees to help, except for Marcel.

He waves his hand in the air and says if they need somebody to sign autographs and take pictures with all the ladies, he'll be there. Marcel always thinks he's something, just because everybody in town knows his daddy owns Willy Q's Barbecue.

I could pound Marcel's face into barbecue with one hand if I wanted to.

"All right," Collins says, just as the bell rings.

"Anybody who wants to be part of this project, be here after school on Monday." As I'm sliding out the door in the middle of the other kids, Collins holds up my notebook and calls out, "Detention on Monday or here, James. Your choice."

Yeah, right.

Like I got any choice.

RHONDELL

All the way home on the bus in the rain, I roll the word *tetrahedron* around in my mouth. I keep my face turned toward the steamed-up bus window, and I let my lips try the word over and over without using my voice. *Tetrahedron.*

I wonder if this is one of those words that might get me into college someday. It sounds as if it could. Inside my mind, I keep a whole collection of college words for someday. Words like *epiphany, quiescent, metamorphosis* . . .

My mom says it's okay to have dreams about going to college, but a person must face reality, too. Reality is that nobody we know has ever gone to college, and we don't have any money to go with, and you have to be very, very smart or very lucky to get in.

Sometimes I imagine college as a big wooden door where you have to knock and say the right password to get in. Only people who know big words like *metamorphosis* and *epiphany* are allowed inside. So, I think I try to save all the words I can because maybe deep down, I believe they will somehow get me inside college without money or luck.

But around here, if you talk and act like you have dreams, or as if you think you are better than everybody else, it only causes trouble. So, I keep most of my college words locked up in my head, and I try to make it through each day by saying as few words as possible. "She's quiet" is the way most people describe me, and I figure being quiet is just fine because it means you won't be bothered.

As the bus rattles down Washington Boulevard with everybody shouting and shoving past my seat because I'm one of the last to be dropped off, I draw a little tetrahedron in the window steam with my finger, and I try to decide if being in Mr. Collins' contest will get me a step closer to my dream or not.

MR. COLLINS

When I am asked why I started the tetrahedron project, I usually — but not always — give one of the following answers:

1. I don't know exactly why.

2. I had been reading an article about the California school and their math record.

3. I was frustrated with my teaching, my school, my students, myself.

4. I was approaching my limit — or in mathematical terms, convergence.

5. All of the above.

Sometimes I also admit that although starting the project was my idea, I never really expected any of my students to show up — and I didn't have a plan when they did.

SHARICE

Six people are already in the math room when I get there on Monday. This kinda surprises me a little. I take a look around the doorway first 'cause if it's only me and Mr. Collins, I don't plan on sticking around. But then I see Ashlee and Deandra from math class. They are hanging all over Terrell (how desperate can you be?) and passing a bag of chips back and forth.

Marcel is there, too, acting like his usual self. He's sitting on the edge of Mr. Collins' metal desk, banging a rhythm on the side of it with his shoes. And James is in the corner near the windows not paying attention to anybody, with his head down on his desk and the hood of his gray sweatshirt pulled up.

Since I'm not crazy about Marcel (and definitely

not James), I slide into the desk next to Rhondell and thunk my backpack on the floor.

"Hey, girl," I say, trying to be friendly even though Rhondell is a real hard person to figure out. She's plain-looking, but not in an ugly way, and she's smart, but not in a lord-it-over-your-head way, and she's friendly, but not in a real friendly way.

"Hi, Sharice," she says, glancing up quick from the book she's reading and then back again. To tell you the truth, it kinda surprises me that she actually knows my name, because Rhondell is one of those people who seem like they wouldn't be bothered with knowing people's names at all because they have too many other important things to think about.

I take a stick of gum out of my purse and unwrap it slowly. Mr. Collins' math room isn't much to look at. First of all, it's on the third floor and the ceiling leaks, so there's always a couple of garbage cans in the middle of the room with the words DO NOT MOVE written on them in permanent marker. And the blank walls drive me crazy whenever I'm sitting in class. If it was up to me, I'd fix the ceiling and hang up something (anything!) and that would be a big improvement.

I can't decide if coming to the math room is going to be any better than hanging around the Washington Boulevard Public Library day after day with the librarians giving me their usual over-the-nose stares and asking me if I have some school stuff I should be working on.

You see, foster non-parent #5 (Jolynn) doesn't allow anybody at home when she isn't there, and since she isn't there most of the time, I'm not allowed to be there either. Which is why I mostly end up sitting in the blue plastic library chairs or in the mall food court, or riding around on the city bus (or wherever I can find a seat without too many weirdos or drunks around).

After I pop my gum into my mouth, Mr. Collins comes into the room. His face doesn't look real thrilled to see us. He goes straight to his desk and starts shuffling through his stack of papers and books like he always does before he starts teaching. This better not be a rerun of math class, I think to myself.

Finally, he looks up, clears his throat, and says, "So all of you are here to build a tetrahedron, right?"

"No," a muffled voice calls out from the corner of the room. "Don't want to be here at all. Don't care about no stupid geometry."

Mr. Collins doesn't answer James, but I notice his face gets a shade more red.

"Well, this is the first time I've tried something like this, so all of us are going to learn this as we go along," Mr. Collins continues in a not very confident-sounding voice. "I'm going to put a chart up on the board and we'll get started." Then he turns toward the chalkboard and takes about ten minutes to draw a big chart, using a yardstick to make every line perfectly straight and erasing any place where they cross over.

Mr. Collins is one of those white teachers who looks like he never gets out in the sun much. He's soft-looking in terms of muscles and kinda thin and his light brownish hair is always parted too far to one side in my opinion.

He writes the words "TETRAHEDRON TEAM" at the top of the chalkboard, and puts each of our names, first and last, on the chart. Of course, he spells my name with an E — Sherice, the same as he always does. I just shake my head and think Sh-A-rice. AAAAAAA. How come you can teach math and you can't remember a simple thing like that?

As Mr. Collins fills in his chart, I get the feeling that he doesn't have a clue about how to run after-school clubs. I've been in just about every club there is, because being in one means you don't need after-school daycare, and if you don't need after-school daycare, it means your foster non-parents can keep more of the money they get for you.

So, I've been in a spelling club, a cheerleading club, Brownies (foster non-parent #2 was Head Brownie), dramatics club, and even a hairstyle club. I'm almost an expert on clubs, you know.

When the teacher finishes our names, I put up my hand. "You gonna elect a Secretary and a President next?" I say. "Because I'm good at being Secretary."

Mr. Collins rubs his nose and says, "Sure, all right, let's do that," and he writes "Secretary" next to my name without even taking a vote. Marcel says he'll be President, and Terrell wants to be Vice President.

"And I want to be Vice President to the Vice President," says Smart Mouth from the corner of the room. The teacher doesn't even argue with James. He just writes "V.P. II" next to James' name.

I keep trying to help Mr. Collins, even though I don't know why.

"Maybe we should make a list of supplies for the project," I suggest, "and I can write them down." Since I don't know the first thing about building tetrahedrons, I get out a sheet of paper and wait for the teacher to tell us what we'll need.

"Glue," he says.

I look up. "What kind — Elmer's glue? Rubber cement? Or glue sticks?"

"I don't know. We'll have to see," Mr. Collins answers in an uncertain voice. I don't think he does crafts very much.

"What else?" I ask, writing a neat number two on my list. I'm a very neat person because most foster non-parents don't like messy kids. So I keep my clothes folded in the drawers and my bed always made. (Hey, at least it gives them one nice thing to say about me.)

"A pattern. Some type of tetrahedron pattern."

"From where?" I ask.

Mr. Collins rubs his eyes. "I don't know. I'll have to find one."

All right, number three.

"Scissors," Mr. Collins says. "And heavy paper."

I write "scissors" and "paper" carefully on my list. "What color paper?" I ask.

Deandra shouts out, "Red, red, red!" like it's the last color on earth. White's cheaper than colored paper, I try to say, because I know a lot about how to get along on not much. For instance, nobody would notice that my shirt is about two years old and a hand-me-down from one of my old foster non-sisters. I always iron my shirts with Jolynn's iron so they will look almost new.

"What do we care about money?" Deandra shoots back at me. "If we're gonna be famous, who cares?"

From the back of the room comes James' voice again. "Rainbow-colored," he says, just being a smart mouth. "Why don't we get rainbow-colored paper?"

"All in favor of using rainbow-colored paper," I say. (Because it isn't that bad of an idea, you know —

why not use all different colors if money doesn't matter?) And everybody votes in favor except James, who doesn't vote at all. He tugs his hood tighter over his head and mumbles that we are a bunch of losers. Marcel tries to tell him to chill, but he gets a punch in the arm for being dumb enough to say that to James Harris. Mr. Collins shuffles through his papers and pretends not to see any of it.

Even with James Harris in the club and Mr. Collins not knowing much about running one, I have a good feeling about it as we get up to leave. I figure that working on something (even math) has got to be better than sitting in the mall or the Washington Boulevard Library, day after day, waiting on Jolynn. You never know — maybe I would turn out to like the math club so much, foster non-parent #5 would have to come looking for *me*.

Now wouldn't that be a real change?

MARCEL

Marcel the Magnificent, that's me. After our math club meeting, I head on over to the Barbecue. Slap a big slab of ribs on a plate. Take fifteen orders at the same time.

"How you want your ribs done, ma'am, heat or no heat? Hot sauce or mild?"

"We got Blast Off to Outer Space Hot, Melt the Roof of Your Mouth Hot, Tar in the Summertime Hot, Red Heels Hot, Mama Thornton Sings the Blues Hot, and Just Plain Ol' Hot. Which you want? Yes, ma'am. Two Singing the Blues coming up. Napkins and forks on the right side. Fire hose on the left. We aim to please at Willy Q's Barbecue. You have a good day, too, ma'am." I slam the order window shut.

Ahhh. Feet up. Butt down.

My daddy, who everybody calls Willy Q, looks over from the grill, where he is sweating and melting like tar in the summertime. He mops his face with a towel. "Who said you could take a break?"

"Homework," I say, pointing. "I got English. History. And a whole lot of math. Going for a world record in math."

My daddy thunks the grill lid down and wipes his hands on his old blue apron. "Willy Q's Barbecue is going for the world record, too," he says. "Three hundred dollars in sales today. Willy Q's Barbecue is hot, hot, hot. You sell two more Singing the Blues, Marcel, and we are set for the night. We can go home and eat a pizza."

He points at the school stuff beside my chair. "Why you got so much homework? Ain't you been doing your work in school? And why you so late getting here to work today? You in some kind of trouble?"

On the back of an order pad, I do a quick sketch. "We got a new math club at school," I tell Willy Q. "Trying to break a world record. They elected me Prez. Gonna take different colors of paper and make them into little shapes that look like this." I hold up my drawing. "See?"

"That's a pyramid," my daddy says.

"No." I show him. "Tetrahedron. All triangles, see?"

My daddy smacks my arm. "Don't you get too smart for Willy Q's Barbecue," he tells me. " 'Cause we don't need smart, we need sales."

He crosses his arms and squints at me. "How long this club gonna last, Marcel? You got a job to do — hope you ain't forgetting that."

I give him Marcel's special Turn-on-the-Charm-and-Give-Them-the-Big-Pearly-Whites smile. Same smile I use for when the grill's too slow or we got too many people waiting in line. "Ain't gonna last very long, teacher says. Not that long."

Willy Q don't fall for that smile, though.

"Better not," he warns, getting up and going back to the grill. "Break's over. Get back to work, Marcel."

Singing the Blues
Barbecue Sauce

¼ cup brown sugar

½ cup ketchup

⅓ cup white vinegar

4 tablespoons olive oil

¼ cup water

2 tablespoons Worcestershire sauce

½ teaspoon salt

¼ cup molasses

2 tablespoons lemon juice

2 tablespoons sweet hot mustard

Combine all ingredients and bring to a boil. Simmer 15 minutes, stirring occasionally until sauce is sweet and singing the blues.

MR. COLLINS

Math problem to solve:

Each level of a tetrahedron increases by a factor of four. So, in order to build a bigger tetrahedron, the students at Washington Middle School will need to add a new level and make four times as many pieces. If the California tetrahedron had 4,096 pieces, how many pieces will the Washington Middle School students need to make?

JAMES HARRIS III

Forget this. That's what I feel like telling Collins. We're sitting in the guidance office and Collins says that I'm going to fail math for the first grading period because I'm not passing his tests or turning in any of the homework. He shows me all the empty boxes in his grade book.

Like I care about those empty boxes.

"I'm very concerned about you," he tells me. He puts on that sad-eyed look that teachers use to show they're concerned when they're really not. They're just worrying about handing out too many F's and looking like bad teachers.

I stare at the window behind Collins and think about how good it would feel to jump out that window and send all that glass flying into the air like one of those jagged comic book pictures with the word *CRASH* written above it. Get out of school, Collins' class, all the other dumb teachers' classes — and never come back.

Collins says if I start coming more often to his math club after school, he might let me pass the first grading period with a D. "We need a lot more help with the project," he says, leaning back in his chair and waiting for me to answer. "So, James, what do you think? Would you consider doing that or not?"

I think about telling Collins — gimme an F. That I'd rather fail. That I don't feel like doing his dumb math homework or making his dumb pyramid, either. Most days, I got better things to do after school than sit with a bunch of losers. Even Terrell says he's thinking of dropping out because the girls are nothing special to look at.

But I decide to play Collins' little game. "How many days a week do I have to keep coming to the club to pass math?"

The teacher's eyes waver, like he hadn't thought of being asked this question. "Every day you don't turn in your math homework," he answers finally.

"And how long I gotta stay?"

"Well . . ." Collins' eyes glance toward the clock. "Four o'clock, how about that?"

"Ain't staying past 3:45," I reply, staring out the

window again. "I got a life, you know, and it ain't here in school."

Collins shakes his head and gives me the sad-eyes look again. He starts into a long speech about how he wishes he could make me see that my life would be so much different if I realized that school was a way out.

"You've got such a talent for art," he says. "Don't you see that? You could go to college someday, or art school. . . ."

I've heard this speech from teachers so many times I could give it myself. What they don't get is, I don't like school, and I'm already good in art and there's nothing else I feel like learning about it. They should see the wall of drawings I got at my uncle's place if they think I need to learn something.

I snooze and count sheep in my head until Collins finishes.

"Can't stay until four," I repeat again when he's done talking. "Gotta be home by four. I got rules."

That rules excuse was just a lie, of course. I didn't have no rules. Not one. Me and my brother, DJ, lived with our uncle, who didn't care what we did. The real reason that I had to be back by four was that DJ and his friends always showed up at my uncle's place around then and sometimes they'd let me hang out with them, if they didn't have plans — plans meaning something they didn't want me being a part of.

Most of my brother's friends were the kind of people you wouldn't want to mess with if you saw them on the street, especially Markese. He'd been kicked out of school already for the stuff he'd done. Wouldn't that be nice, right? But the others were cool to me. When they saw me in the hall at school, they'd slam into my shoulder and say "Hey, little brother — wake up, what's happening?" Two more years and I'd be the one slamming into shoulders just like DJ and the others. The hallway would move apart to let me pass —

Collins closes his grade book with a thump, which brings me back to where we were at. "All right, James," he says with a sigh. "If you keep coming to the math club and stay until 3:45 — not 3:30, or 3:35, or 3:42 and a half — I'll give you a passing homework grade. But just for this marking period. And you have to show up every day the club meets, do you understand that?"

"Ain't coming on Saturday and Sunday," I say. "No way."

Collins gives me a look. "You know what I meant."

As I walk out the door, I can't help grinning to myself and jumping up to high-five the top of the door frame. "See ya later, Mr. Collins," I call out. "You have a good weekend now."

See, Collins may be a math teacher, but he ain't very smart. All I said was that I would show up from 3:00 to 3:45. Didn't agree to do nothing for the club. So I could waste forty-five minutes drawing comics in the back of the classroom, and he'd still have to let me pass math. Man — DJ and his friends would say — you a genius.

And I was.

MR. COLLINS

Another math problem to solve:

If seven students and their math teacher worked on building the giant tetrahedron from 3:00 to 4:00, Monday through Friday, and each person made about 30 small tetrahedrons an hour, how long would it be until they reached their goal of 16,384? Extra credit: What if it is not that easy?

WILLY Q

Nothing gets past Sergeant Willy Q. Williams.

I'm a Vietnam vet, so I seen it all, you know what I mean? I was in the Army for fourteen years. So I know a thing or two about kids. Seen kids not much older than my son go to war, get shot up, and die. That's what I'm always telling Marcel. He may think he's smarter than me. He may think he can pull the wool over my eyes — but nothing gets by Willy Q. Williams.

When I see Marcel coming in late to work again — the third time in a week — I pick up the phone we use for taking orders and call his school. I ain't gonna listen to another smooth excuse about why he's late. I know the streets and I know everybody in this neighborhood, good and bad, and I'll find out where he's been and what he's been up to, and he'll think twice before lying to me again. And if he's doing drugs or hanging out with the wrong crowd, he'll be sweating over the grill at Willy Q's Barbecue for the rest of his life.

A lady answers at the school.

"Good afternoon," I say, "this is Marcel Williams' father, Willy Q. There a math class meeting there?"

The lady says no, not that she knows about. There's basketball practice and cheerleading; that's all.

I start counting on my fingers. One lie.

"There a Mr. Collins there? A math teacher?"

I wait for her to say no, there's nobody named Collins either. But she says hold on, she'll page him on the loudspeaker. A customer walks up to the take-out window, but I tell him to hang on and I stay on the line waiting. When Mr. Collins finally picks up the phone, I can tell right away that he's a white guy. About forty or fifty years old maybe. Least that's what he sounds like.

I tell him I'm calling to check if my son is in an after-school math club of his, because that's what he's telling me, and I want to find out if that's true or not. And I have to admit that it surprises me a little to hear the teacher answer yes, it's true.

"What's the purpose of this club?" I ask. "Does Marcel need extra help in math? He failing or something?"

Mr. Collins says no.

"This for some kind of test that kids need to graduate?"

Mr. Collins says no.

"This just some kind of self-esteem club like they're always pushing these days, to make kids feel good about themselves?"

Mr. Collins says no, the kids are learning geometry and trying to break a math record set by a school in California.

Same story Marcel gave me.

"Now, maybe some kids have time to stay after school and break math records, but my son doesn't." I say this in a respectful tone of voice, though. I tell Mr. Collins that if it wasn't for our barbecue place, me and my son wouldn't have a roof over our heads or food in our mouths. I can't run the place alone, I explain, not with how much business we get. I need my son here every day, helping me after school. I expect that you can understand that.

Mr. Collins tries to make me change my mind. He wants me to let Marcel stay for the club once or twice a week. "Maybe you have some days that are slower than others," he tries to argue. "Marcel is a big part of the team, and we'd hate to lose him."

I tell the teacher that I'm a Vietnam vet and being a soldier taught me that responsibility always comes first. Marcel's responsibility is to work at the Barbecue. When you're a soldier, you learn to do what you have to do, not what you want to do, and that's the way I'm trying to raise my son, I say.

"Now" — I glance over at the customer who is getting impatient — "what time is school dismissed every day, Mr. Collins?" After he answers 3:25, I thank him for speaking to me and tell him to be sure that Marcel leaves school at that exact time each afternoon. "I'll be waiting right here for him," I finish.

MARCEL

I got Slow Burn Sauce cooking inside me. The kind of sauce that gets hotter after you swallow it. Hotter and hotter. Like flames licking up the inside of a house.

We don't aim to please nobody at Willy Q's Barbecue, ma'am. We got the worst food in the whole state of Ohio. Maybe the entire world. No hot sauce. No mild sauce. Nothing. You have a terrible day, too, ma'am, and don't you ever come back.

That's what I'd like to say.

Instead I smack some ribs over on the grill and slop sauce on them. Won't look at Willy Q. Won't talk to him neither. Let him disappear in a puff of smoke. Wouldn't care.

Ain't spending the rest of my life working at Willy

Q's Barbecue. Saying sweet things to customers who don't deserve sweet. Smiling like I care about selling rib bones and chicken wings and pig meat.

Ain't joining the Army either, like my daddy thinks. Won't salute nobody. Least of all, him.

I'm gonna be a comedian. Or a Hollywood actor. Here comes Marcel Williams. The movie star. Can't you hear them saying that? Big black stretch limo. Hot girls on each arm. Ain't he something? they'll say.

Willy Q doesn't want me staying for the math group anymore. He says I gotta be at work every day by 3:30. Mr. Collins bent the truth about what time school lets out, just to get my daddy to believe that. "But at least you can stay with us for twenty minutes or so after school," Mr. Collins said, trying to make me feel good.

Twenty minutes.

The Slow Burn Sauce starts bubbling inside me again. I can feel the heat rising. Maybe I'll work harder in those twenty minutes, Willy Q, than in all the hours I'm working and sweating for you —

Willy Q hollers at me. "We got a customer, Marcel. Over at the window. You watching out or not?"

I open the order window real slowly and give my best I-Don't-Really-Care-What-You-Want-to-Order smile.

Good afternoon, ma'am, I say inside my head. You better order real fast because Marcel Williams ain't gonna be here too long, no matter what his daddy thinks. He's gonna leave this place and be a star. . . .

"We got Blast Off to Outer Space Hot, Melt the Roof of Your Mouth Hot, Tar in the Summertime Hot . . ."

Marcel's Slow Burn Sauce

½ cup ketchup

¼ cup water

1 tablespoon brown sugar

½ tablespoon lemon juice

1 tablespoon vegetable oil

½ teaspoon cayenne pepper (or more for hotter taste)

1 tablespoon Worcestershire sauce

½ teaspoon dry mustard

¼ cup white vinegar

¼ teaspoon red pepper flakes

Combine all ingredients, bring to a boil, and simmer for about 15 minutes. Makes about 1 cup of sauce. When served, this sauce will be very hot with a slow burn that takes its time cooling down.

SHARICE

Mr. Collins' club is falling apart right in front of his eyes, and he acts like everything's fine. Hey, Mr. Collins, I want to wave my arms and say, this club is getting smaller and smaller, or haven't you noticed? Like pretty soon it's just gonna be me, Rhondell, and you, if you don't do something about it.

"You should try bringing snacks," I tell him one afternoon when nobody else shows up except me and Rhondell. "It's too long to wait from lunch until we get home and the school lunch is usually some kind of mystery meat, so half the time we don't eat it anyway. That's why most clubs have snacks."

After that, Mr. Collins starts to bring in bags of chips and popcorn. Sometimes his wife sends in something sweet like homemade chocolate chip cookies or fudge brownies — just like my mom probably would have made for me every day after school if she was around. I don't think foster non-parent #5 has made a cookie in her entire life, so I'm always trying to slip an extra one or two into my purse to eat later. (You know, pretend my mom or Gram made it for me.)

Even though foster non-parent #5 is causing me more and more problems, I don't talk about them with anybody. (LIKE, I DON'T HAVE TO SHARE EVERYTHING THAT IS MESSED UP IN MY LIFE.) I just keep on acting like my smiling, friendly old self.

At least kids start showing up for the first half of the club now, before the snacks run out. We stand around Mr. Collins' desk eating our handfuls of pretzels or potato chips, and drinking the cans of pop that Mr. Collins lets us sneak from the pop machine in the teachers' lounge, if we've got quarters — or he gives out loans if you don't.

We can usually count on Marcel and James and sometimes Terrell and Deandra being there. Ashlee doesn't come anymore now that she finally woke up and got herself a new boyfriend. Me and Rhondell are always there, of course. Mr. Collins calls us the Dynamic Duo. I don't like the name much, but I think he is trying hard (too hard, if you ask me) to act like a more friendly teacher to us, and so I let it go.

Mr. Collins says he still remembers how quiet everybody was on the first couple of days we worked together. Me and Rhondell were hunched over our desks, trying to get the pieces to fold on the lines and stay glued. Which was impossible. About halfway through the second day, I remember looking over at Rhondell and she had blobs of glue all over her desk and one of her pieces had just come unstuck again and the two of us almost fell over we were laughing so hard — like it was the funniest thing to see that orange piece she'd been holding for about twenty minutes suddenly come flying apart. That's when I knew we'd get along okay.

We're faster now, of course, but we're still not making much progress on building the giant pyramid. Like no progress. "If we were Egyptians, we would have been fired, girl" — that's what I tell Rhondell. In my opinion, most of it is Marcel's fault because he's the president of the club and he hasn't been sticking to his job. He eats the snack and leaves halfway through the club — what kinda president is that?

So, I decide it's time to tell Marcel that even though I like him a lot (not like as in LIKE, like as in — he's ALL RIGHT to be around), we need somebody new for president. If people are going to come to the club and eat snacks, they have to do the work, too, I say. And if the president can't stay for the whole time and help build, then somebody else should take over, or we're never gonna break the world record. (It's already the beginning of November.) I tell Marcel that I'm willing to volunteer to fill in for him.

But I think everybody just about choked on their pretzels when James jumped into our conversation and said he wanted to be the president instead. We were standing around Mr. Collins' desk and he came strolling over to us with that sly, sneaky grin of his and announced, "I'm already Vice Prez, right? So I'm the next in line to be Prez before any of you except Terrell, who's not here, so that means I should be the new Prez, doesn't it?"

We tried to argue with James that he hadn't done any work, so how could he possibly take over everything. But he said we were all wrong about him.

"I got more talent than any of you," he said. "Way more talent."

I couldn't believe it when Mr. Collins took his side and agreed to give James a chance. See, Mr. Collins doesn't have a clue about kids. That's his problem as a teacher. Other teachers would have seen right through James. They would have known he was trying to pick a fight with Marcel like he picks fights with everybody. James is just plain mean and I don't know why Mr. Collins couldn't see that. He just lets him butt on in and take over.

"Girl, this whole club is gonna fall apart now," I say to Rhondell as we walk down the hall after school. "You mark my words. He'll ruin the whole thing. Why would Mr. Collins *do* something like that?"

Rhondell is silent. I figure she doesn't want to tell me that it was really my fault for opening my mouth about us needing a new president. See, she's smart and I'm not. She knows when to keep her mouth shut and I don't. (WHY CAN'T I EVER LEARN THAT?)

I should have just left things the way they were. See, that was always my mistake. I was always trying to fix things — like trying to make my foster non-parents be nicer people or trying to act better so they would like me more. One time, I had a foster non-parent who used to lock up every room in her house at night because she was afraid of foster kids stealing from her, so I told her it would save her a lot of trouble if she waited to see if I was honest first instead of wasting her time locking everything up. Just suggesting that idea got me into trouble with her.

And if I had left things the way they were years and years ago, maybe I wouldn't even be living with foster non-parents in the first place, because maybe my Gram would still be alive. In fact, you could probably say that if I hadn't been born when I was, things could have been different. Maybe my mom wouldn't have gotten into that car to get away from her screaming, throwing-up baby (me). . . .

As Rhondell pushes open the front door of the school and we step outside, the first snow of the year is falling. Actually, it isn't really snow, but more like round spitballs zinging out of a freezing gray sky.

"Look at that, Sharice," Rhondell says, squinting up at the sky. But I'm so mad at myself, I just duck out into the snow without saying good-bye to Rhondell or even stopping to pull on the sweatshirt I've got in my backpack. I head down the street toward the library, letting the spitball snow sting my arms.

JAMES HARRIS III

"This pyramid's gonna have STYLE now that I'm working on it." That's what I tell the group on the first day I'm Prez. "And everybody better do exactly what I say now that I'm Prez, too. Or else you gonna get a beating from me."

"James —" Collins raises his eyebrows and gives me the teacher look, but I just pretend to ignore it. I stroll on over to the big pyramid that Marcel and Collins have been starting to glue together, and I show them how they don't have a clue about what they're building.

"Why you gluing the colors like that?" I point to a section where little purple and green and yellow tetrahedrons have been all mixed together. "You should be gluing the same colors next to each other — you know, make one big section of purple, then blue, then green" — I show them with my hands — "so the whole pyramid looks like a rainbow when it's done. That would make more sense than this mess —" I wave my arm at the pyramid.

See, I've been sitting back there in my corner drawing my comics and watching them try to build this pyramid for about a month now — and it's been cracking me up because Collins can't build and Marcel doesn't know what he's doing when it comes to art. Just look at his daddy's barbecue signs. I could have given them about fifty ideas for how to make the pyramid look better, but they didn't ask me for help, did they?

I got the idea for making the rainbow a while ago. I was sitting there in the back of class doing nothing one day and I remembered something I did in art class when I was in third or fourth grade. The art teacher, who was this cool guy who sometimes played music

in class, had us soak this heavy piece of white paper with water and then paint big stripes of different colors. The water on the paper made the colors blend together like a rainbow, and once the paper dried, we did pen and ink drawings on top of it. Mine was a bald eagle with its wings out. It was one of the best things I had ever done, and I wished I still had it, but I didn't. Who knows where all that stuff went?

But I figured if the tetrahedrons were glued together by color, they would blend into a rainbow just like that painting did. Even though nobody else looks like they agree, Collins says he likes my idea, and since the pieces are only attached at the points, it wouldn't be too hard to pull apart the glued ones and rearrange them. We haven't gotten too far on building anyway, he says — and that's the truth.

So that's how I start turning the project around. Trust me, Barbecue Face Williams never would have thought of this rainbow idea, if he was still being Prez.

Every day, I stay later and later at school, trying to keep everybody doing what they're supposed to do and not messing up the colors. Afterwards, I ride home on the bus, still trying to peel the dried glue off my fingers. Sometimes I don't get back to my uncle's apartment until way past 4:00. Come dragging in, half-starved, and find DJ and his friends hanging out in the living room, with their cans and cigarette butts lying around everywhere. Don't know why they can't pick up nothing.

"Hey, Math Boy," they call out, "go out and find us something to eat."

I'm not sure what's up with DJ these days, but he's getting a real attitude. Like he's turning into somebody I don't even know. We always used to look out for each other. When we first came to our uncle's, I remember the two of us sitting on the beds in the apartment and my brother saying that even though it was just the two of us now, I could always count on him as my family. He was serious, too, which he almost never is. Then he told me the story for the hundredth time about how he was the one who carried me up three flights of stairs by himself when I was about four or five and fell on the sidewalk outside the apartment where we lived back then and cut open my forehead.

These days, I figure he'd probably just leave me facedown on the cement.

I think that's why I keep spending more and more time with the math club. Because DJ isn't acting like anybody I'd call family — or anybody I'd even call related to me — and I'm tired of getting ordered around by him and all his friends.

Or maybe I just like being Prez and telling everybody else what to do.

RHONDELL

Quiescent. I saved that word from a poem we read in English class, and although it was used to describe caterpillars curled up in their cocoons, I liked it. I sometimes feel like a caterpillar hidden inside a cocoon, even though my Aunt Asia often tells me I need to consider changing how I am around people. Aunt Asia is my mom's younger sister. She works as a stylist at the Style R Us hair salon, and she's the kind of person who doesn't mind talking to anybody and everybody. I think she probably wishes my mom and I were more like her, but I believe that being quiet and hidden means you sometimes notice things that other people don't.

One of the things I've noticed after coming to Mr.

Collins' math club since the end of September is how people are different than they seemed at first. For instance, I've worked with Sharice since the first day, but I've learned that she is somebody who has some very odd beliefs and superstitions about things, which you don't realize until you spend time with her.

"Purple — now that's my good luck color," she always says when we're working together, folding and gluing the little tetrahedrons. "Hand me all the purple." The first time she said it, I asked her why purple was her good luck color and she gave me an annoyed look and said, "What's wrong with having a favorite color, Rhondell? Don't you?"

There are other colors she won't touch. I have to fold all of the yellow and blue, for example. "Get that paper away from me, Rhondell," she'll tell me, pushing a stack across the desk. "Those colors are bad luck for me. Real bad luck. Don't even let me look at them."

But how could certain colors be good luck or bad luck to somebody? I wonder. And why?

Marcel is different than I expected, too. Even though everybody always thinks he's good-looking and smooth, if you really watch him, you'll notice that he acts like he's nervous deep down. His brown eyes flicker around the room when he's talking to you, and his foot taps up and down, and he never sits anywhere too long — he perches like a jumpy bird on the heater, or on the teacher's desk, or on the edge of a chair.

He and Mr. Collins are usually the ones who take our little pieces as we finish them and join them together to make the larger tetrahedron. It takes steady hands to glue the pieces together point to point. Maybe because his whole body seems like it is always moving and balancing on the edge of something, Marcel is better than anybody at doing this.

But *metamorphosis* is the college word I'd pick for James. For weeks, he showed up after school and wouldn't help with any part of the project. He sat in the corner near the windows, with his big feet propped on the chair in front of him, and drew in his notebook or spun quarters on his desk until they flew across the room and hit the walls or the front of the metal heater, making all of us jump. My mom would have called him trouble with a capital *T*.

And then overnight, he turned into somebody else. Once he became president, he started bringing in his sketches of how the tetrahedron should be built and where all the colors would go. His idea was to make the pyramid look like a rainbow. Even though everybody thought he wasn't being serious at first, that he was trying to be rude to Marcel by making him take apart everything that had been done, now I can see what he meant — how the colors are supposed to blend into each other.

But sometimes I wonder if James Harris has really changed, or if underneath his pretending to care about the math club and being president is the same person. He still calls Marcel "Barbecue Face," and me "Ron Dull," no matter how many times Mr. Collins warns him about not using those names. And Sharice told me she heard that James' father is in jail for drugs and he lives with his older brother, who has been in trouble for drugs, too. They're bad news, she says.

Could someone who is bad news really change that much? For a math project? Was it a metamorphosis or something else?

SHARICE

I'm the one who comes up with the idea for the Christmas party.

Sometimes when we're working, this silence will come over the room when all you can hear is the buzzing of the fluorescent lights or the clanking of the old heating pipes, and if it goes on for too long, it kinda makes me crazy, you know?

Maybe it reminds me too much of the Washington Boulevard Library, or of sitting in the hospital room next to my Gram, when she was sick. So I'm the one who always tries to keep the conversation going. When it gets too quiet, I just pull a question out of thin air — whatever pops into my head, whatever I want to know right at that moment. Why do fluorescent lights buzz? Is the new English teacher dating the gym teacher? Why does it get dark so fast in the winter?

"I got a question, Mr. Collins," I'll say in the silence, making my voice a little louder on purpose, and everybody will crack up, except for Rhondell, who usually just bites her bottom lip to keep from smiling too much and looks the other way.

"Yes, Sharice," Mr. Collins will answer from somewhere on the other side of the big tetrahedron, where he's working. "What's on your mind?"

"What about a Christmas party?" I ask one afternoon.

The snow's coming down like pillowcase stuffing outside the math room windows and maybe that's what gives me the idea. Or maybe it's the Christmas music I've been listening to every day in the mall, that won't get out of my head now. ("Have a holly jolly Christmas" . . . you know, what does that really mean anyway???)

"Don't you think having a Christmas party's a good idea, Rhondell?" I kick her chair leg with my foot, trying to get her to agree. Rhondell glances around in her usual way before she says sure in a non-sure voice.

Marcel jumps in. "I can bring all the food," he tells us. "Whatever you want. Ribs. Wings. Sandwiches. My daddy's got the best barbecue in the whole state of Ohio —"

"Yeah, right," James snorts, even though everybody pretends not to hear him.

"Sure, okay, why not?" Mr. Collins answers, breaking into a big smile (which you don't see very often from him in class). "Let's have a Christmas party."

So we start planning who will bring what — the food, the dessert, the decorations, the plastic plates and cups, the drinks, the music. James is the only one who doesn't offer to bring anything, because he says he isn't coming. We try to convince him that the president has to be there, but he says a Prez doesn't have to do anything he doesn't want to do. A Prez has got better ways to spend his time than going to girlie Christmas parties, he says.

The rest of the day, I can't keep my mind from thinking about the party. I plan about a hundred different ones in my mind. The last real party I remember being at was one that my Gram had for me when I was six or seven. She brought home a cake from the grocery store. It was a Snoopy cake because I loved Snoopy back then, and she gave me the silver necklace with the little cross that I still have (way too small to wear now), and some of the kids from her church came.

That night, as I'm riding around and around on the city bus waiting for Jolynn to get home, I spend so much time thinking about the party that I almost forget to get off the bus when it passes by our stop for the fifth time at about eight o'clock, and I have to jump up and tell the bus driver to let me off at the next stop. Walking back to Jolynn's house in the slushy snow and the pitch-black winter darkness, I've still got "Holly Jolly Christmas" playing in my head.

MARCEL

I wait until Willy Q's in a good mood to tell him about the Christmas party. The Lots-of-Orders-Making-Us-Lots-of-Money good mood. This time of year, that's Friday and Saturday nights. I wait until after he's counted up our money and he's cleaning up the kitchen.

"My class is having a Christmas party after school next week," I say real smooth. Don't mention a word about the math club being the reason.

Willy Q doesn't look up. "What's that got to do with me?" he says. Like he knows exactly what I'm gonna ask next.

Maybe I shoulda waited for the Saturday good mood.

"They were wondering if Willy Q's Barbecue could send over something. Just for the party. Something little to try."

"Ain't a charity," Willy Q answers, scrubbing the pans harder.

I give Willy Q my best Turn-on-the-Charm-and-Big-Pearly-Whites smile. "They heard we got the best barbecue in the whole city," I say.

"We does." Willy Q shrugs. "So what?"

The Slow Burn Sauce starts bubbling inside me again. I think about answering, so what would you do if I told you I ain't working for you anymore? Or what if nobody ordered your tasteless old barbecue — not on Friday night or Saturday night or any other night?

Instead I say, "So maybe we should show them we do."

Willy Q crosses his arms and turns toward me. "Bet they haven't tried some of our new barbecue wings, now have they? Or some of that good Southern cornbread I've been making?"

I don't tell Willy Q that his cornbread ain't all that good. Cannonball Cornbread, that's what I call it. Too heavy. Shoot it out of a cannon and a chunk of

Willy Q's cornbread could wipe out half the city of Cleveland.

Willy Q reaches for one of the order pads. "How much food you need and when?"

Even though I tell Willy Q that the party's only for about five or six people, he says he'll go ahead and send food for ten. When the math club sees all the food Marcel the Magnificent is lugging to the party, they ain't gonna believe their eyes. Cornbread. Wings. Short ribs. Cake —

"Don't want folks to think we're stingy," Willy Q insists.

Take my advice. Don't try to figure out Willy Q. Just grab what he gives you and run. That's what I do.

WILLY Q'S CANNONBALL CORNBREAD

1¼ cups flour

¾ cup yellow cornmeal

2 tablespoons sugar

½ teaspoon salt

1 tablespoon baking powder

½ teaspoon dry mustard

dash of nutmeg

1 cup milk

1 egg, beaten

¼ cup margarine, melted

¼ cup onion, finely chopped

1 cup canned white shoepeg corn, drained

Preheat oven to 425 degrees. Grease 9-inch square pan. In medium-sized bowl, combine flour, cornmeal, sugar, salt, baking powder, dry mustard, and nutmeg. Mix well. Stir in milk, egg, and melted margarine. Lightly mix in onion and corn. Spoon batter into greased pan. Bake at 425 degrees for 20 to 25 minutes or until toothpick inserted in center comes out clean. Serve warm. Cover and refrigerate leftovers. Trust me, there will be a lot.

JAMES HARRIS III

Maybe I'll come to the party and maybe I won't. I don't make my decision until I'm walking past the classroom at the end of the day, already wearing my coat to leave. I shove my hands in my coat pockets and slow way down to listen to what's happening before I get to the doorway. I ain't staying to sing with any karaoke machine or play any stupid party games, if that's what's going on. That ain't me.

But the only thing I can hear coming out of the room is whining country music. I stick my head in the doorway just to call out, "Who's listening to that sicko country music?" And then Collins comes over wearing a party hat that has a turtle on it. He looks like a complete fool. The hat says HAPPY 10TH BIRTHDAY, even though this is a Christmas party and Collins isn't ten. "Come in and join us, James." He waves his arm at me.

"Ain't listening to that music," I answer, shoving my hands deeper in my coat pockets and leaning against the doorway, staying right where I am.

"Well then, find some music you like, James," Collins answers in the same happy white voice, pointing toward the boom box. "Just come in and have something to eat." Then he heads back over to the table where the food is set up.

If it was up to me, I'd rather sit on the other side of the room and work on the project. We're only about halfway to the top, and we got a bunch of blue pieces waiting to be glued together. But working on the tetrahedron doesn't seem to matter to nobody but me. Sharice and Rhondell are laughing themselves silly and taping Christmas streamers everywhere — stringing them around Collins' desk and across the top of the chalkboard. Marcel and Collins are leaning against the heater, stuffing their faces with barbecue. Terrell and Deandra squeeze past me, carrying two heaping plates of food in front of them. "Sorry we can't stay.

Gotta go catch the bus." Terrell waves to Barbecue Face. "Thanks for all the good food, man."

Still not making up my mind about staying, I walk over and check out what's left to eat. Marcel pushes a plastic plate into my hands as if I'm standing at his daddy's barbecue window or something. "Try some of our wings." He buzzes around me like a fly that needs swatting.

"And the ribs." He points. "If you like hot sauce, try the ribs. Tar in the Summertime Hot, that's what me and Willy Q call them —"

I give Marcel a hard stare. "Get outta my face, fool. I can pick out my own food."

But I gotta admit that after all the fast food and pizzas and boxes of cereal we eat at my uncle's, maybe I forgot how good real food tastes. I take four big pieces of chicken. Ribs. Wings. Pile them on my plate like a barbecue mountain. When I pick up the ribs with my fingers, I can feel my fingertips burning, I swear. And by the time I've eaten about half the food on my plate, my whole body is breathing heat. I have to open my mouth to let out the smoke.

"Stuff's pretty good, man," I hear myself saying to Marcel.

Maybe it's all the food, or Collins getting rid of the country music on the boom box and playing some rap, but I stay longer than I planned. I been to worse parties; let's just say that. We stand around the food table, talking about all kinds of things. Sports. Music. Movies. Collins is up-to-date on his movies, even though he doesn't have a clue about basketball. Doesn't even know everyone who plays for Cleveland. How could you not know that?

But when Sharice starts running her mouth about how our math club is like its own little family, I have to get up and leave. We're all sitting around eating Marcel's chocolate cake when Sharice looks up. "We're kinda like a little family, aren't we?" she says, smiling and licking frosting off her fork. "Mr. Collins is like the head of the family. And the four of us — me, Rhondell, Marcel, and James — are like the kids. And Terrell and Deandra are the second or third cousins who show up out of the blue every once in a while, right?"

Makes my skin crawl to listen to her. Who would

picture our math club as a family? What's this girl thinking? That's what goes through my mind.

"You crazy," I say, pulling my coat off the back of the chair and putting it on, because I'm not sticking around any longer for this kind of talk. "Gotta get going," I say. "Bye." And then I'm out the door.

I sprint past all the empty classrooms, locked up for the night. The only sound you can hear is my shoes slapping on the tiles. In my mind, I draw a picture of big footprints disappearing over a hill like they show in cartoons. The farther away I get from Sharice's idea of a Christmas party, the better I feel.

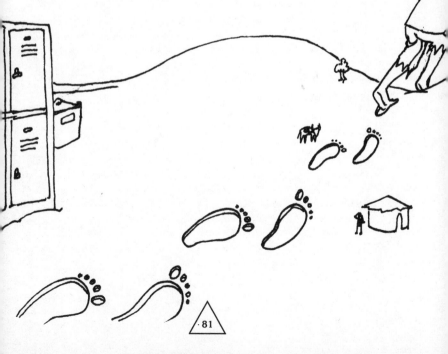

SHARICE

After James leaves, nobody speaks at first. I'm feeling real embarrassed for saying what I did (WHY DON'T I EVER LEARN?), but then Marcel jumps up and says, "Maybe the Prez don't want to be family with us, but here's the real question — who wants to be family with him?" And that makes everybody start laughing. Marcel reaches for the plastic cake knife and twirls it between his fingers. "Anybody want more cake to eat, because I do. . . ."

While we're stuffing ourselves with second pieces of cake, I ask Mr. Collins to tell us more about his family. "How old are your kids?" I ask him, through a mouthful of cake.

He takes out his wallet and shows us their pictures.

"Here's Emma." He points to a picture of a little girl with curly blond hair and a round pie face. "And that's Max," he says. The boy in the next photograph is older, maybe ten or eleven, and has Mr. Collins' thin face, brown hair, and serious look, no doubt about it.

"Is he good in math?"

"Terrible." Mr. Collins smiles and shakes his head. "He's like his mother, more into music and computers and that sort of thing."

"And what was that first picture in your wallet?" I ask.

Rhondell gives me one of her stop-being-so-nosy looks. But I can't keep from being curious about people, you know. As Mr. Collins was turning to his kids' pictures, I couldn't help seeing the black-and-white picture of somebody's face in the front. All I wanted to know was who it was.

Before Mr. Collins turns back to the picture in his wallet, I hear him take a deep breath and let it out slowly (like maybe I shouldn't have asked to see any more). But then he holds up the picture and everybody leans closer to get a look at it. It's a small photograph of a teenager in a military uniform. His face is serious, but he's good-looking, you can tell.

"That's my brother Jerry," Mr. Collins continues in a quiet voice. "He was a soldier in Vietnam." And just the way he says that sentence makes your stomach suddenly turn over and you don't even have to ask the question to know that his brother is dead.

"He doesn't look that old," I say, feeling uncomfortable. "How old was he in that picture?"

Mr. Collins closes up the photographs carefully and puts his wallet away. "Nineteen," he answers in a soft voice. "Old enough to die in Vietnam. At least the people who sent him to war thought he was."

"My daddy is a Vietnam vet," Marcel adds, acting prouder than he should, I think, especially after somebody has told you that their brother died in the same war.

But Mr. Collins just replies, "Well then, you've heard a lot about it."

"Willy Q wants me to go into the military just like him." Marcel shakes his head. "Ain't doing that, though. No way. I'm gonna be a movie star. Or a comedian."

I try to change the conversation to something else. I pull another question out of the air. "Did you always want to be a math teacher?" I ask Mr. Collins.

He stands up and brushes the cake crumbs off his shirt. "After my brother died, I did," he replies.

When Marcel asks him why, Mr. Collins says it was because math had answers when life didn't. "In math you can solve problems and find solutions," he explains. "There are rules and patterns. Like the tetrahedron." Mr. Collins points in the direction of our half-finished one. "But when your older brother dies in a war and you're only twelve years old, there aren't any solutions to find. Somebody dying when he's nineteen years old on May fourteenth in 1969 on a hill called 937 in South Vietnam — those numbers in life don't have answers, they don't make sense, no matter how hard you try to understand them."

There's a long, uneasy silence after he finishes talking until Marcel jumps up nervously and shouts, "Why we talking about this serious stuff, all of a sudden? Making me DE-pressed. I thought this was a CHRISTMAS party!"

"Yes, you're right, it is." Mr. Collins puts on a big smile and walks over to the boom box. "Let's get some Christmas music on and talk about something else."

But later, when we're loading up Mr. Collins' car with leftover food and party stuff, I can't keep my voice from starting to tell him the story of my mom and Gram. (Maybe Marcel doesn't understand what he meant, but I do.)

"I lost my mom when she was nineteen, too," I say as we're walking down the hallway and the other two are way back of us. "So I know what you mean about math and life."

Then, before I can stop it, I hear my voice pouring out the whole story. How my mom went out riding in a shiny blue sports car the night she died. How I'd been sick and colicky, my Gram said, and I'd spent two solid days and nights screaming and crying until nobody wanted me anymore, least of all my mom, who was still young and not ready for a baby at all, especially not wrinkly-faced, screaming me. "Just going out for a drive with some friends and getting something to eat," she told my Gram. "I'll be home before eight."

But she never came home. The cops knocked on Gram's door about nine that night and asked if she had a daughter who had gone out riding with two friends in a dark blue car. When Gram said yes, they told her that the car had been racing down the road, lost control, hit a pole, and all of them were killed. All three people. Every time Gram told this story, I always blamed my mom's death on the blue car. I don't know why. (Maybe it was easier to hate a car than people.)

I tell Mr. Collins that Gram raised me until her heart began to act up. That was the phrase she always used — "act up." It started with trouble catching her breath. I remember how I would fly up the dark wooden steps in her house, taking them two at a time, and I'd stand at the top waiting and she would go up three or four steps and have to stop to rest. "You and your young legs," she would say, trying to smile in between coughing and fanning her face with her hand. "Not sure I can make it all the way up there to tuck you into bed tonight, honey pie."

And then, it wasn't long before she couldn't even go up the steps. She slept on the couch in the living room wrapped in the bright-colored crocheted afghans she liked to make, and I was the only one who lived in the upstairs rooms. When I was seven years old, she had to be put in a hospital, and she died in that same hospital just about a month later.

But I leave out the other part of the story — which is the fact that I was the one who called for the ambulance that took her to the hospital in the first place. If I hadn't done that, maybe everything would have just continued on like always — me running around the upstairs rooms, playing magic castle and building forts, and Gram sleeping under her crocheted quilts downstairs.

I also don't mention the bouquet of yellow flowers either. When the nurse sat down next to me in the waiting room one morning and told me that Gram had left for heaven during the night, I was holding a bouquet of yellow daisy flowers I had planned on giving to her that day. I remember staring at those yellow flowers and hating them with all my might, because it seemed to me those flowers must have known Gram was gone and just let me go ahead and buy them anyway.

Yellow and blue had been my bad luck colors ever since.

After the whole story pours out of me like a river that can't be stopped, I feel afraid right away. I had never told anybody about my Gram and my mom before. (What is my problem?) But Mr. Collins seems to understand some of what I'm saying, I think. "That's a hard way to go through life, I know, Sharice," he says, quickly patting one hand on my shoulder like an uncomfortable father. "I felt the same way about my brother, very much the same way. It isn't easy — still isn't easy."

I know this sounds like a strange Christmas party, but to tell you the truth, it was a really good time. When I walked down the street to the bus stop after the party was over, I felt lighter. My mind was full of Christmas songs, and chocolate cake, and red and green streamers. And for the first time I had told somebody the story of my mom and Gram, and I felt better about that, too.

(I should have known that the feeling wouldn't last long.)

MARCEL

Nobody eats barbecue in January. That's the truth.

It's teeth-chattering, spit-freezing weather. Me and Willy Q huddle in the back room. Try not to freeze to death from cold and boredom. Parking lot covered in about a foot of snow. Order window jammed shut. If anybody comes up to order — which almost nobody does — I gotta put on my coat, push my shoulder into the side door to get it to open against the snowdrifts, go around the building, and take their order. I always give them my What-Kind-of-Crazy-Person-Would-Want-Barbecue-When-It's-Ten-Below look.

You poor kid, they usually say. Does your boss make you come out here and take orders without any hat or gloves? Yep, I always nod, while my fingers turn into blue icicles writing down their order. Maybe they won't come back again, I figure. Child abuse, you know.

Willy Q spends most of the day hunched over on his stool, squinting at the little black-and-white TV on the counter. He watches all the talk shows and worries about how much money we aren't making. "Pack your bags, Marcel," he'll tell me about every half hour. "I hear them coming to evict us." Worst month in all the years he's been doing business, he says.

Always been the worst month. Every January. Don't say that to Willy Q, though. Ever since that conversation in math club about Mr. Collins' brother dying in Vietnam, I've been trying to be nicer around him. That conversation in math club got me thinking: No Willy Q. No me.

Maybe I'm trying to show him I'm glad he kept himself alive in Vietnam, so I could be alive, too. I don't know.

"How about making up a new sauce?" I say on one no-customer afternoon.

Willy Q's eyes flicker from the TV to me. "What's wrong with the sauces we got?"

I shrug my shoulders. "Just trying to think of something new," I tell him.

Willy Q snorts. "We don't need new, we need sales."

He goes back to watching TV and I go back to doing a half-finished crossword from an old newspaper I found sitting on top of the meat freezer.

But it isn't long before Willy Q turns toward me again. "What kinda sauce were you thinking of?"

I tell him we need a winter flavor. Nobody wants Tar in the Summertime in January. Can't even see tar. Or blacktop. Or anything but snow in January.

Willy Q snaps his fingers. "Snow in January Sauce. That's it."

The rest of the afternoon, me and Willy Q make a mess of the back kitchen, trying to cook up a winter barbecue sauce that's white. We pull out just about every bowl in the place and mix together all kinds of crazy ingredients. Willy Q starts pulling stuff off the shelves and out of the refrigerator, left and right. Mayonnaise. White vinegar. Milk. Cream of tartar. Even a handful of snow.

Man, that's awful, we laugh and choke and cough,

trying a taste of everything. A few times we nearly fall over, laughing so hard. When I spit tartar and mayo sauce all over my shirt, Willy Q has to stop for air and wipe the tears out of his eyes.

We never do get a good Snow in January Sauce made. But like Willy Q says, it don't matter. Least it keeps us from freezing to death. Or going crazy.

RHONDELL

Maybe I notice things about Sharice that no one else sees. Nobody else seems to realize how different she is after coming back from Christmas vacation. Before vacation, she asked unstoppable questions and talked more than anybody else except my Aunt Asia. She organized the Christmas party, and we did all the decorating together. But after coming back, she is mostly silent and lost somewhere inside herself. She is like one of the small tetrahedrons after they are folded up and glued together. *Withdrawn* is the college word I'd use for her.

I wonder if there is something wrong in her family. Maybe somebody who has let the devil take hold, as my mom says about families who fall into drinking or drugs. But then I realize that even though I've told her all about my mom and how she is a religious person who directs the Sanctuary Baptist Church choir on Sundays, and I've talked about my dad who left when I was two years old, and I've even told her about my Aunt Asia (who wears gold nail polish and has different hair every time you see her), Sharice has kept herself a mystery the entire time.

I don't even know what kind of family Sharice has. I can't remember whether she ever talked about a mom or a dad or even other brothers and sisters. In fact, the only thing I know about her family is the street where they live — Fifteenth Street, because she takes the number 209 bus with me sometimes and I see her turn the corner there when she gets off at the stop.

"Is there anything bothering you?" I try to ask her one afternoon at math club when we are sitting down to work. The words come out of my mouth nervously.

"No. Why?" she answers, and I can't think of what to reply except to say that she seems different all of a sudden. Her eyes flash me a look of suspicion. "What's wrong with different?" she asks.

A day or so later, while we are riding on the school bus, I try to find out more about her family. I choose a question carefully and ask it while I'm talking about my mom's job at the downtown hospital and all of the hours she works. "Where does your mom work?" I inquire, as if it is just an ordinary question. But Sharice turns her face toward the bus window and tells me that she doesn't like talking about her mom.

There are other things I notice, too, and I feel embarrassed for noticing them — as if I'm being prying, and I don't think that's a good word to be. But I can't help noticing how Sharice's face is too ashy-looking and dry and her eyes are shadowy and tired, as if she's staying up way too late. Her hair isn't kept up the way it used to be, either. It straggles out of its twists in fuzzy wisps that she's always reaching up and trying to smooth down with her hands.

In math club, she acts strangely now whenever we are ready to leave. After we walk outside, she is always forgetting something in the building and asking Mr. Collins if she can run back to get it — her purse, her homework, her keys, her gloves. . . . "Don't wait for me," she'll tell us.

Each time, Mr. Collins sighs and shakes his head. "You need to be more organized, Sharice. I shouldn't let you back in the building if I'm not there." But she'll always duck inside the door fast, before he can say any more. "I'll remember next time," she always promises. Only she never does.

Sometimes I have the feeling that Sharice is hiding more secrets than any of us really knows.

MR. COLLINS

An important fact to remember about tetrahedrons:

Although the large tetrahedron appears strong and stable, it should be noted that its pieces are joined together only at the smallest of points. The edges and faces remain largely separate and unconnected.

JAMES HARRIS III

My brother's friends start in on me the minute I walk through the door one afternoon. I check out the living room but there's no sign of my brother DJ. Course that's nothing unusual with DJ these days. Three of his friends — Anthony, Markese, and Leon — lounge on the floor with CDs and burger wrappers scattered all around them.

"Where you been, little brother? You late," Markese says, grinning and looking at me with his sharp switchblade eyes. He is half-crazy on drugs most of the time. You don't mess with Markese because you never know.

"Nowhere, man," I answer, trying to slip past them into the kitchen, without looking like I'm slipping past.

Anthony throws a wadded-up hamburger wrapper at my back. "Hey, you still working on that math thing with Collins? That why you late all the time?"

"Why?" I answer, cutting my eyes back at him.

Another burger wrapper nails my back. "Hey, just asking. Chill."

But the switchblade eyes are curious now. Markese sits up and leans back against the couch. He folds his arms across his chest. "What math thing?" he says in a slow voice.

I can feel my stomach tighten up exactly like it does before a fight or when you think somebody is about to come after you. Last thing I want to be doing is talking about a school math project with Markese.

"Nothing," I answer, trying to duck out.

But Anthony, who's in eighth grade at Washington because he flunked a year, jumps in and gives Markese all the details. He tells him how Collins' classroom is building something that looks like a pyramid. "It's different colors, and they're trying to break some world record, that's what I heard," he says.

Markese's eyes slide over to me. "That true about

the pyramid?" he asks, with a curious smile spreading across his face.

I shrug. "Maybe. Who knows?"

Markese's eyes sharpen. "Can anybody go and see it?"

"Yeah, whatever . . . ," I answer, trying to say as little as I can, but still saying too much, I feel like. Like I said before, you don't want to mess with Markese.

"Hey, if you wanna see it sometime, I'll get you into the school." Anthony grins, looking over at Markese. "You know me. I'm up for anything —"

Even after I go into the kitchen, the three of them keep on talking and laughing behind me. The warning feeling stays in the pit of my stomach. I pour a big bowl of cereal that I don't feel like eating and tuck a can of Pepsi under my arm.

In the room that me and DJ share, I shut the door, put on my headphones, and turn up the music as loud as it will go. Stretching out across my bed, I smack open one of my notebooks and start drawing whatever comes into my head. I do a whole page of clenched fists — ones that are getting ready to slam into somebody's face if they get too close. I'm good at drawing hands. Half of my notebooks are filled with them. But no matter how many fists I draw slamming into windows and walls and faces, I still can't get rid of the bad feeling I have about Markese.

SHARICE

I get tired of always finding excuses for staying later, so finally I ask Mr. Collins if I can work extra on the tetrahedron, after the math club leaves. I make up a big story and tell him how my foster mom's hours at work have suddenly changed and nobody's home until five or six. "My neighborhood's real dangerous with break-ins and all," I say. "It's safer here."

The truth is that Jolynn isn't coming home until midnight or later some nights because she's out with her new man. "Better stay with some of your school friends tonight, Sharice," she'll holler from the bathroom while she's doing her hair in the morning. "I'll be out late again."

"I'll just come home when you get back," I always insist.

"It'll be awfully late, honey," she'll answer. "Sure you don't want to stay overnight at your friend's house if you're already there?"

What friend's house?

I don't know what Jolynn thinks I'm supposed to do. I have friends at school, but not the kind I want knowing all my business. For instance, what would Rhondell think if I turned to her and said, "Girl, would your mom mind if I stayed over your house this week because foster non-parent #5 isn't coming home?" So I try to stay at school as late as I can, and then I usually find another place to sit for the rest of the time.

Mr. Collins says if I'm going to stay later, I have to be out of the building when the basketball team leaves at six. And it's my responsibility (he stretches out this word to emphasize how important it is) to turn off the lights and pull the classroom door shut when I do. "Twist the knob and make sure it's locked." Mr. Collins shows me.

But I never leave anywhere close to six o'clock.

Usually it's seven or eight. A few times, even nine o'clock. The custodians don't come upstairs to clean until way after eight. I know because I asked one of them, "What time do you get to cleaning the third floor?"

The old custodian, Mr. Joe, covered his mouth with his hand and whispered, "Girl, with all there is to do in the place, sometimes we don't ever get up to the third floor." (Which you could tell by looking around, I guess. Same chocolate bar wrapper stuck in the same water fountain for a week sometimes.)

I've got my own little way of doing things, once everybody in math club leaves. I turn off the first two rows of lights and ease the door shut. Mr. Collins' door has a shade, so I pull that down, too. No one can tell I'm sitting inside the room because I've stood in the hallway and checked.

After that, I take my supper out of my backpack and set it neatly on a white paper napkin as if I'm sitting in a fancy restaurant. Usually supper is half of whatever I had for lunch (a squashed cheese sandwich, or tater tots wrapped up in a napkin — something like that), a soda pop, and a candy bar from the vending machine. I prop my feet up on one of the desk chairs and eat slowly to make it last.

After I'm done with dinner, I try to work on my homework a little to keep my Gram happy in heaven (because you know she's probably watching). Although there are always some nights when I can't make myself care, and I take out my homework, look at it, and slide it back in my bag without doing a thing.

After that, I fold the little tetrahedrons and listen to music the rest of the time. It's the only part of the day I like, to tell you the truth. When I'm sitting by myself in the math room and my fingers are flying (folding, gluing, folding, gluing) and music is playing in my ears, I can't worry about all of the things that are going wrong in my life, so maybe that's why I like it.

The tetrahedron is getting closer to the top every day — mainly with all my extra work. We're only a few thousand pieces away from finishing. Everybody's always asking me how I get so many done, and I have to bite my tongue to keep from telling them if they were at school until eight or nine, they'd get a lot done, too.

I like looking at the big tetrahedron at night when nobody's around. I walk around it, squinting at the colors and spaces from different angles, fixing places that have come unstuck here and there. At night, the colors seem to glow more than they do during the day — shimmering purple, red, orange, yellow — one color blending into the next, like James said they would.

Sometimes I turn out all the lights and perch on the top of the heater, tilting my head from one side to the other, studying the pyramid. With the streetlights shining through the iced-up classroom windows behind it, the tetrahedron changes from paper triangles into something that looks more like lace. It reminds me of the point of a big snowflake, the way it looks so delicate and fragile in the darkness.

If I stare at it long enough, sometimes I can kinda pull myself inside that tetrahedron snowflake, and imagine all the starry edges and points floating in the air around me. I can drift through the night sky just like one of the tumbling snowflakes outside, thinking about my mom and my Gram who died, and everything I don't let myself think about during the day usually. (Good thoughts, not bad ones.)

And maybe that's what happened on the last night of January when I drifted out of the room without remembering what Mr. Collins told me to never forget. I left for home at about seven o'clock, and I never turned back to check the door.

MR. COLLINS

In random number sequences, it is impossible to predict the number that will come next. There is no pattern. What happened to my students' math project was random and patternless in the same way. It was early on a Wednesday morning when Joe Hill, our school custodian, stopped me at my classroom door. He told me that something had happened during the night. That someone had broken into the math room and vandalized our project. Nothing of the tetrahedron — not a single piece, he said softly — was left standing.

RHONDELL

There are no words — college words or any words — for what I feel when I see the empty space where the rainbow tetrahedron used to be, and look at the crumpled pieces of paper covering the entire floor, and remember how hard we worked to make those pieces every afternoon for months. It is as if everything shrivels up inside me, like a caterpillar turning to dust inside its cocoon. I stand in the middle of the room, still holding on to my books, trying to understand how it could be gone.

Next to me, Sharice is silent. Even Marcel, who is always teasing and joking, has a frozen look on his face.

Mr. Collins tries to talk to us about what happened. "I know all of us worked hard on this project and this is very difficult —" His voice catches in his throat and he has to pause. "Very difficult to understand . . ."

He looks around the room helplessly. Everything is covered with shreds of colored paper. Even some of the textbooks have been torn apart and trampled. "I don't know why somebody would do this. . . . I just can't explain why anybody would be so cruel as to come in and wreck a project like this, when all of us were just trying . . . to do something good."

James can't handle hearing any more than that. Out of the corner of my eye, I see him suddenly turn while Mr. Collins is talking, pick up one of the desks, and slam it into the others. Another desk tips over and crashes to the floor, making us all jump. Then, without a word, he runs out of the room, punching his fists into the lockers, all the way down the hall.

Mr. Collins tries calling out for him to stop. He goes into the hall and tries to order him to come back, so we can sit down together and talk over our feelings and figure out what to do. Doors all along the hallway open as teachers and kids look out to see what is happening — but nothing stops James. Even the security guard in the hallway doesn't dare to get in the way of James' out-of-control self.

As James' punches echo down the hall, Sharice crouches down to the floor and begins to carefully gather up the torn pieces. I watch as she scoops up handfuls of purple and yellow and green pieces and puts them into her backpack. What is she thinking? I wonder.

"Why you doing that, Sharice?" Marcel snaps. "Just forget it. Just throw all those pieces out." He moves toward the door, kicking at the piles of torn paper. "Just throw the whole thing out."

Tears are flowing down her cheeks and her nose is running, but Sharice just keeps wiping her nose on her sleeve and scooping up piles of paper and dumping them into her backpack, as if she believes she will be able to put them back together.

I pick up a handful and try to convince her it won't work. Maybe Mr. Collins will start the project over again next year, I tell her, and you and I and Marcel can work on it again. But she just shakes her head and orders me to get away from her. "Leave me alone, Rhondell," she says. "You don't know anything about what happened."

Mr. Collins can't get her to listen either.

"I'm gonna rebuild it," she tells him stubbornly. She just keeps repeating the same four words — I'm gonna rebuild it. She doesn't stop until her whole backpack is full of colored paper. Then she zips it closed and slips it over her shoulder. "I'm going back to my English class now," she tells Mr. Collins, even though I don't think she does, because we have English class together at the other end of the hall, and I hear her feet go down the steps instead.

After Marcel and Sharice leave, I help Mr. Collins and the custodian sweep up the rest of the room. We fill up four garbage bags of dreams.

SHARICE

Sitting on the back steps of Jolynn's house, leaning against the screen door, I watch the snow fall like torn paper out of the gray sky. The snowflakes land on the legs of my jeans and melt, land and melt, until the tops of my jeans are soaked clear through, and I don't care at all.

Nobody else knows what I did, but I do. I'm the reason our project was torn to pieces. I'm the one who was in the math room when I wasn't supposed to be there, and I'm the one who didn't lock the door. And if you want to go way back again, I'm the reason why my mom died in a car crash and I'm the reason why my Gram went to the hospital and died, too.

Rhondell was right. Nothing's gonna fix those

torn pieces, you know. Not all the glue in the world. I pull out a handful from my backpack and look at all the colors jumbled up together. I think about how close we were to finishing. Maybe only two or three weeks or so. I remember how that tetrahedron looked in the darkness. Just like lace and all. A big tower of lace.

Opening my fingers, I let the handful of paper scatter onto the snow. Little flecks of red, blue, green, and purple fall around my feet. I reach down and pick out a crumpled lavender piece that lands near my shoe. Opening it up and smoothing it on my knee, I can still see the triangle shapes we folded over and over.

The purple paper always reminded me of my mom's dress. In my bedroom upstairs in Jolynn's house, I keep a small silver-framed photograph of my mom wearing a purple dress. It's a little out of focus, but you can still see it's a nice summer dress with thin straps over the shoulders. My mom was a pretty woman — stick-thin, but pretty, Gram always said. The picture was taken at the Methodist church picnic, and it's the last one I have of her. She's wearing dark sunglasses and sitting between Gram and one of Gram's old friends, with her chin resting on her hand, like she's looking at something far away. I'm in a baby carrier half in and half out of the picture.

I watch the snowflakes fall on the lavender paper, watch it melt into a piece of soft lavender fabric in my hand, just like my mom's summer dress. I curl my bare fingers around that fabric, holding on.

It's snowing heavier now, and everything in Jolynn's backyard is getting covered — the empty doghouse, the crab apple tree, and the rusty refrigerator leaning against the garage. Won't be long before the snow covers me up, too.

Closing my eyes, I lean back against the door of Jolynn's house. I'm not going anywhere — not to the bus station, or the library, or the school. Not anymore.

AUNT ASIA

Rhondell's mom is my sister, but we are about as alike as hot peppers and sweet potatoes, or lemons and honey — if you know what I mean. Don't get me wrong, I love my sister to death, but we are not the same people. She walks around with the weight of the world on her shoulders, and probably the rest of the planets, too. I just take things as they come. Easier that way, you know?

Anyway, I'm just finishing up my last client at the Style R Us salon — old Mrs. Jenkins, who has hair as coarse and dry as a wire brush — when Rhondell calls. Now, since my sister works at the downtown hospital and taking care of sick folks isn't as simple as rescheduling haircuts, I've always been kinda like a second mom to Rhondell. If she needs to be picked up from school or gets locked out of her house — which Rhondell almost never does, of course, being as smart as she is — she's supposed to call me at the salon. "You just give me a ring, honey," I'm always telling her. "Any time of day. It don't matter. Poor folks' hair can wait, but my only living niece can't."

I'm always pestering her to do something with her hair whenever she calls, too. Rhondell's plain-looking, but that doesn't mean something can't be done to plain. Come on in and let me fix up your hair for you, I try and beg her. We could put it up, or press and curl it — whatever you want, hon. Everybody needs a new look.

But like mother, like daughter, I guess. Rhondell's been wearing the same pulled-back, head-hugging hair as long as I've known her. Still, hope springs eternal. I pick up the phone, thinking maybe this time, maybe she's gonna start growing up and caring about her looks.

"What can I help you with today, Miz Rhondell?" I say, balancing the phone on my shoulder and holding up one finger to tell Mrs. Jenkins to wait just one minute.

"Are you busy?" Rhondell asks in a soft, serious voice, just like her mother. "If you're busy, Aunt Asia, I can call back some other time."

I squint out the salon window at the falling snow. "You stuck at school? Once I'm done with Mrs. Jenkins, I can come on up there and give you a ride home, hon. You don't need to be wandering around catching cold in this kind of weather."

But Rhondell says no, she doesn't need a ride, she's calling for advice about a friend of hers. I almost drop the phone, to tell you the truth, because in all the years I've known Rhondell, she has never once called me about any friends, at least none that I can recall. Although I've asked her about friends so many times, I finally gave up and decided to save my breath.

I told my sister that Rhondell's shyness was something she should look into, and my sister said she had enough to do, and shyness was better than some things she could name. Like mother, like daughter, again.

"What kinda advice you looking for, hon?" I say, trying not to sound too pleased at being asked, while giving Mrs. Jenkins another glance.

"Something happened at school today, to a project we were working on . . . ," Rhondell says. The story comes out slowly, with a lot of hesitations and pauses, and I don't follow a lot of it, but I don't push her for more.

"A girl who works with me left the school right after it happened," Rhondell continues. "But even before this, there was something wrong with her, I think. I don't know exactly what, but I was wondering, well —," her voice hesitates, "maybe what to do now."

This is more words than Rhondell ever says usually, so I'm jumping for joy inside my head at the same time that I'm trying to decide what to answer.

I tell Rhondell that if it was me, and if the girl was my friend, I would give her a call first. "I had lots of girlfriends in school, Rhondell — and we called each other all the time. About big things, little things. We were always there for each other, you know what I mean?"

But, knowing Rhondell like I do, it doesn't surprise me at all when she says she doesn't even have the girl's phone number.

"Where's she live? Near your street?" I ask. "Maybe you could try stopping by her house. You know, just go on over and ask how she's doing."

Rhondell says she thinks the girl lives on Fifteenth Street, but she doesn't feel right stopping by. "I'll just wait until she comes back to school to talk to her. Thanks, Aunt Asia. I'm sorry for bothering you at work —"

"Hold on now —," I call out. Old Mrs. Jenkins reaches up and pats the uncombed side of her wet hair, giving me a tight-lipped, impatient look. "After I finish with Miz Jenkins here, I'll drive you over to the girl's house to check on her; how about that?" I say.

"No, that's all right —"

"I'll come around about five. No trouble at all. Drive right past Fifteenth on my way home. Gotta go now, hon, see you soon."

Sometimes the hot peppers have to tell the slow sweet potatoes what to do, I tell myself as I hang up the phone. If somebody doesn't start pushing Rhondell, she's never gonna have a soul in this world except me and her mom, and what a pair we are, you know what I mean?

Next thing I'm gonna insist on changing is her hair.

RHONDELL

Even though it is snowing hard enough to be a blizzard and Aunt Asia is wearing heels and a dress, she still insists on driving me down Fifteenth Street to find Sharice's house. I watch her gold-painted fingernails tighten on the steering wheel as the car wheels slip and slide in the snow.

The college word for Aunt Asia is *determined*.

"We should turn around and go back," I try to tell her. "I'll just talk to Sharice next week."

"Don't be silly," she answers, leaning closer to the windshield. "We're having fun, aren't we?"

The windshield keeps filling up with snow even with the wipers going full speed, so Aunt Asia rolls down her window to try and see the house numbers on Fifteenth. She calls them out as we pass: 345, 347, no number, can't see, 365 . . .

I keep hoping that we don't find the number I told her, the one I got by calling the school, because I haven't even thought about what to say to Sharice if we do find her house. What will she think when she opens the door and sees somebody from math club standing there?

But then Aunt Asia shouts, "There it is!" and our car slides into the driveway with a soft crunch of snow. I'm not sure we'll ever get out of the driveway again, by the way the car sounded. Aunt Asia cuts off the engine and we peer through the windshield at the house. It's a worn-looking two-story brick house with an old front porch in need of painting. All the windows of the house are dark. "Nobody's home," I say, hopefully.

"You can't ever tell," Aunt Asia answers. "Maybe their electricity is out. Maybe they don't keep up with their bills. Could be that's one of your friend's problems. Maybe her family's fallen on hard times. Families do, this time of the year. Don't I know it." She rolls her eyes. "Half the business I usually get — gone, this time of the year."

Aunt Asia fiddles with the heater. "I'm gonna sit right here keeping warm, and you go up there and check if she's home. Come and get me if you need me, Rhondell." She smiles at me and pats my arm. "You'll do fine, hon. All you have to be is a good listener."

I want to sit in the warm car with Aunt Asia and not go anywhere. I stare at the house number on the paper in my hands and try to decide what to say to Sharice, if she answers the door. Just checking to see if you're okay. . . . Everybody was worried after you left, so I said I'd stop and see about you. . . . Mr. Collins told me to come by. . . .

Looking up at that house with no lights and the snow swirling around it, I feel as if the house has a big sign saying GO AWAY. KEEP OUT. CLOSED.

"Don't forget to check the back door, too," Aunt Asia calls as I slide slowly out of the car. "Some people don't answer their front doors, you know."

On the front porch, a big pile of rolled-up yellow

newspapers and junk mail fills the space between the screen door and the front door. It looks as if nobody has used the door in months, and the only footprints I can see on the porch are cat prints in the thin layer of snow. I reach my hand behind the broken screen door and try knocking on the inside door, but nobody answers.

As I walk around to the back, I can feel the snow drifting into my shoes and soaking my socks. The yellow headlights from Aunt Asia's car shine ahead of me like two flashlights. With the swirling snow and the darkness of the house and yard, I don't know what makes me notice the bits of colored paper on the snow beside the house. Perhaps the headlights from Aunt Asia's car catch a few of them. But when I see the torn pieces scattered across the snow, a jolt goes through me. My heart begins pounding watch out, watch out, watch out, on its own, as if it knows something is wrong with those pieces being in the yard.

I come around the side of the house with my heart pounding watch out, and that's when I see the dark shape of somebody sitting on the back porch steps. The shape is huddled over, curled up, on the steps. I don't even check to see who the somebody is; I just go slipping, running, flying down the driveway to get Aunt Asia.

MARCEL

"What's up with you?" Willy Q asks me.

"Nothing."

He crosses his arms and gives me the five-minute Willy Q Army stare. "Don't lie to me. Something's wrong," he says. "I can read your face like a book."

"Nothing's wrong."

"Fights? Grades? School? Girl trouble? What's up?"

"Nothing."

"We'll see about that," Willy Q says. He walks over to the counter where we keep the cakes and pies. Goes right to the chocolate cake in the middle. Lifts the round plastic cover. Cuts a slab the size of a sidewalk, plops it on a plate, and pushes it in front of me. Sets a fork next to my hand. "Have some cake," he tells me.

I know better than to eat Willy Q's Chocolate Truth Cake. *Sweet enough to make tongues start talking* — that's what it says on the menu. Willy Q always insists if he coulda made his Chocolate Truth Cake in Vietnam, even the enemy would have talked.

You can see the look in people's faces after they take the first bite. They try the first mouthful of cake kinda fast, and then everything goes into slow motion. Their eyes close. They lick the sweet frosting and cake off one side of their fork. Then, they turn it over and get every last crumb and speck on the other side. "My, that is good. That is REAL good," they say.

And then they start talking.

They tell us about their family. Where they grew up. Who made the best cake, and who didn't. What's going wrong in their life now. Money problems. Health problems. No job. But how a bite of this good cake has made them feel better. Sugar does wonders, they declare. Me and Willy Q just nod our heads. Chocolate Truth Cake, we say, works wonders every time.

But it ain't gonna work for me. I push the cake to the side. Go back to thinking about what happened at school again. How it felt to see all that work torn apart. How it meant that none of us would have a chance at getting our names in the news. Probably be working at Willy Q's Barbecue the rest of my life. Giving folks my big I-Shoulda-Been-in-Hollywood-But-Instead-I'm-Working-Here smile.

Willy Q pushes the cake back in front of me.

"Talked to my friend Joe at your school today," he says slowly. "You remember Joe, right? The one who was in Vietnam with me?"

I nod.

Willy Q leans closer, giving me his Army-interrogator look. "Joe told me some vandals broke into your school and ruined a big project some of the seventh grade kids were working on with their math teacher. He said it was a real sad sight. Don't suppose you know anything about that project, do you, Marcel?"

I shake my head no. Not much, I say.

Willy Q points his finger about two inches from my face. "Don't you keep secrets from Sergeant Willy Q. Williams. I know everything that goes on around here, Marcel. I got eyes and ears in places you don't even know about. That was the project you were working on with those kids, wasn't it?"

"Don't matter now, does it?" I answer.

Willy Q goes over to the Chocolate Truth Cake and cuts another sidewalk slab for himself. He slides it onto the counter and sits down next to me.

"Joe told me you were staying after school and working on that project with those other kids," he says, taking a big bite of cake. "Don't think I didn't know what you were doing. Joe checked it out for me a while ago. . . ."

Willy Q points at my plate.

"Keep eating cake," he says. "Then we'll talk."

WILLY Q'S CHOCOLATE
TRUTH CAKE

1 cup all-purpose flour

1 cup sugar

¼ cup unsweetened cocoa powder

1 teaspoon baking powder

¼ teaspoon baking soda

¼ teaspoon salt

dash of cinnamon

¾ cup milk

¼ cup shortening

1 egg

½ teaspoon vanilla

¼ cup chocolate chips

Preheat oven to 350 degrees. In a bowl, combine flour, sugar, cocoa powder, baking powder, baking soda, salt, and cinnamon. Add milk, shortening, egg, and vanilla. Mix with an electric mixer (medium speed) for about two minutes or until well-mixed. Pour batter into 9" x 1½" round baking pan that has been greased and floured. Sprinkle chocolate chips on top of the batter. Bake at 350 degrees for 30 to 35 minutes, or until toothpick inserted in center comes out clean. Allow to cool for 10 minutes, then remove cake from pan and cool thoroughly on a baking rack. Frost with a thick layer of sweet chocolate frosting and wait for the truth to come out.

RHONDELL

I won't repeat all of the biblical names that Aunt Asia uses as she jumps out of the car and runs toward the back of the house to help the huddled shape I saw on the steps. She follows me, running through the snow in her stockinged feet, with her arms holding her red wool coat tight around her.

When we reach the backyard, Aunt Asia starts screaming, "Wake up, wake up!" at the shape before we even get there, and I am filled with relief when the huddled shape moves and begins to sit up slowly. A head covered by a striped yarn hat lifts slowly and scatters off its layer of snow, and then I can see for certain that the face belongs to Sharice.

"What in the name of Jesus are you doing out

here, sweetie?" Aunt Asia yells, almost nose to nose with Sharice, rubbing her shoulders up and down with her hands. "You gonna freeze to death, don't you know that?" She yanks Sharice up from the steps. "Come on back to our car now. We gotta get you to a hospital or a doctor or something."

With one arm and half of her red coat tucked around Sharice, Aunt Asia runs back to the car with her. Once we get inside, she huddles us together on the front seat and turns the heater on high. Hot air comes pouring out like an oven at the three of us. Going through another list of biblical names, Aunt Asia rubs her feet and stomps them on the car mats, trying to warm them up.

"Get that girl's shoes off," she says to me. "We gotta see if she has frostbite."

But Sharice shakes her head and finally says a word or two. She tells Aunt Asia her feet are fine and she doesn't need to go to any hospital.

"Well, we'll let my sister, Thea — Rhondell's mom — decide that," Aunt Asia insists. She pushes her foot down hard on the accelerator and barrels the car back down the driveway, with the tires spinning and squealing in the snow. "I'm gonna go to your house first, Rhondell, and see if your mom's home from work yet."

When we get to the house, the lights are on and my mom opens the door. She doesn't ask any questions at first, even though you can tell by the look she gives Aunt Asia that she isn't too pleased with her. All Aunt Asia says is, "This is Rhondell's friend, Sharice, and she's just about froze to the bone."

Mom sends me upstairs for a blanket or two while she and Aunt Asia try to pry some answers out of Sharice. Even from upstairs, I can hear them asking questions about where her mom is and what family she has in Cleveland. When I come back down the steps, my mom is settling Sharice into her recliner, with her feet in a pan of warm water and eucalyptus oil, just like she does to her own tired feet after work every day.

"Just keep your feet in there while I make something warm to drink," my mom is saying. Her eyes move over to me. "You keep her company, all right, Rhondell?"

After that, Mom and Aunt Asia disappear into the kitchen and I can hear them talking softly. I imagine they are trying to decide who to call about Sharice, and I can hear Aunt Asia's heels tapping back and forth on the linoleum, pacing while they talk.

I don't know what's polite to ask Sharice. Sitting with my knees pulled up to my chin, I look down at my shoes and weave the ends of the laces back and forth through each other. Is it polite to ask why she was sitting outside in the snow? Whether she's upset about what happened at school — or something else? Should I ask if she wants to talk? Or perhaps she would rather that nobody bothered her and just left her alone.

The smell of toasting bread comes drifting from the kitchen and Aunt Asia returns balancing a tray in her hands. "My old waitressing days coming back to haunt me," she says in a loud, extra-cheerful voice. "Brought you girls some bread and jam and hot chocolate, how about that?" She sets the tray on the end table.

Settling down on the sofa, Aunt Asia stretches one of my mom's flannel blankets over her legs and reaches into her purse to pull out a big pink nail file.

"Did Rhondell tell you that I'm her aunt?" she chatters to Sharice as if she is talking to one of her clients, and I wonder if she's trying to cover up the sound of my mom in the kitchen talking on the phone to somebody.

"I work at the Style R Us hair salon on Washington Boulevard. Did Rhondell tell you that?" Aunt Asia holds her hand at arm's length, studying her nails, and then goes back to filing. "And I keep telling her" — she points the file at me — "girl, you gotta DO something with that hair."

Sharice smiles a little and Aunt Asia keeps going. "Now you have beautiful hair, Sharice, honey. I can tell that, just by looking at you. And I can tell you CARE about your hair, unlike that one." The nail file points again.

Somehow, talking about hair and nail polish makes the difference. Sharice's expression turns from closed up to half-interested. Before long, Aunt Asia is heading upstairs to dig through my mom's old dried-up nail polish collection. She brings back a color called champagne silver, and she and Sharice start painting their nails a silver-white color on my mom's coffee table. I don't say a word about that, even though I know my mom will.

After talking on the phone for a long time, it's my mom who decides that Sharice will stay at our house for the night. She comes into the living room and announces that it's too bitter cold to go outside again, so Sharice will stay over in my bedroom. My room used to be Mom and Aunt Asia's room when they were growing up, so I have their old twin beds. "And Asia," my mom adds emphatically, in the same sentence about Sharice staying at our house, "that's my good table."

It feels strange to have somebody from school staying in my room. After we climb into our beds, I can't fall asleep. I stare at the light from the half-open door and listen to Sharice moving and fidgeting. Each time she rolls from one side to the other, the bed creaks as if it's not used to having anybody sleeping in it, which it probably isn't since it's usually covered with my reading books and school papers.

Just when I think Sharice is asleep because she hasn't moved or stirred for a while, she talks to me.

"You 'wake, Rhondell?" she says softly.

"Yes."

"I was the one who ruined the tetrahedron," she says, her voice sounding half-muffled by her pillow. Her voice pauses, as if she's waiting for me to say something, but I don't know what to answer. I'm startled, I guess. And shocked. And bewildered. Those are the college words for what I feel.

"I forgot to lock the door," she continues. "I was working late in the math room, and I never locked the door. That's how they got in, you know. They didn't break into the room, they just walked right in."

Now I start to understand — a few things, but not everything. I try to tell Sharice that leaving the door open wasn't what wrecked the project. "The people who came through that door were the ones who wrecked the project," I explain to her. "Not the door being open."

"But if the door hadn't been left open, they wouldn't have gotten in."

"They would have found a way."

Sharice seems to think about that for a while. "Maybe you're right," she says finally. "Maybe they

145

would have." Then there's another long pause and she adds, "Thanks, Rhondell, for coming to get me, too."

"Sure," I answer, feeling uncomfortable, even in the darkness.

"How did you know where I lived?" her voice continues.

"I called the school and asked."

"You are so smart, Rhondell," she says. "I never would have thought of that."

"It's not that smart."

"I think it is."

And then it's quiet for a long time, so I guess that Sharice has finally fallen asleep. I continue staring at the ceiling and thinking to myself. The light coming from the hallway makes a skinny triangle shape, like one side of a tetrahedron, on the ceiling of my bedroom — and that reminds me again of how much I'm going to miss the math club.

Although I told Sharice it didn't matter about leaving the door unlocked, I have to admit that it does matter — deep down at least, it does. I know she didn't mean to cause any harm. And I know it wasn't Sharice who tore the project down, it was vandals. But I can't keep my mind from considering the same question over and over: would things have been different if she had just remembered that one little thing?

MR. COLLINS

Four questions of mine that still don't have answers:

1. Who destroyed our tetrahedron project?

2. Why did they destroy it?

3. Should the tetrahedron be rebuilt?

4. And who will do that?

JAMES HARRIS III

I draw eyes all over the back of my notebook — staring sideways at me, staring down at me. Feel like everybody's eyes are on me all the time — Mr. Collins, Marcel, other kids, other teachers, as if they know I've got information I'm not sharing. But I'm not telling nothing. Not even about Markese.

Principal called me into his office and tried to find out what I knew. "Other people here at Washington may trust you, James," he said, leaning across his desk to stare at me. "They may think you've mended your ways. But I know better. You come from a rough crowd, and it wouldn't surprise me if you had some hand in this."

How's telling people like you what happened gonna

help me, fool? That's what I'd like to say to Principal. You gonna snap your fat white fingers and make everything better? Why don't you step into my shoes for a while? I got a brother who's no brother, an apartment with no food, my brother's friends who are just looking for a reason to come after me . . . and that's only the beginning of all my problems. Why'd I be stupid enough to cause more trouble and spill my guts to you?

So I tell Principal I don't know nothing, even though I do.

They try all kinds of bribes and threats to get other kids to talk — all-school detention, canceling a Friday basketball game, offering a $100 reward — but nobody confesses anything because I'm the only one who knows that it was Markese and his friends who wrecked the project, and even though I'd like to see them have to glue the whole thing back together piece by piece for the next fifty years, I still keep my mouth shut.

But in English class, while Clueless Sub is reviewing what we know about clauses, I start thinking about how long it would really take to rebuild. Eight months? Six months?

"James, tell us one thing you know about clauses," Clueless Sub says.

"Santa Claus. That's all I know, man," I answer.

And Clueless Sub says, "Get out in the hall, young man, and don't come back until you're ready to respect my authority."

Yeah, right . . .

So I sit in the hall and try to figure out how many days we would need if we started the project again. I tear off part of a sheet of notebook paper that's sticking out of somebody's locker and pick up a chewed-up pencil that's sitting under the water fountain. It takes me about half an hour to figure out all the dividing and carrying to do. Math ain't my thing, so I don't know why I'm even trying. Nothing else to do in the hall, though, and I'm not going back to Clueless Sub.

My figuring says if we could make 150 pieces a day, divided into 16,384 — the number of pieces needed for the record — it would take us about 110 days. Meaning, if we started now and worked five days a week, we could probably be done sometime in July. Which doesn't seem that impossible as long as you don't look outside and realize it's only the beginning

of February, and there's a blizzard outside, and half the winter is still left to go.

At lunchtime, I go and find Mr. Collins. He's eating lunch at his desk.

"This right?" I say, pushing my paper in front of him.

"What were you trying to figure out?" he asks, squinting at my scrawled numbers.

"How long would it take to rebuild? Is a hundred and ten days right or not?"

Collins gives me a strange look, like he's surprised at something, but I don't know what.

He folds the paper in half and hands it back to me. "Think about how hard it would be to start all over again," he says, beginning to clean up his lunch. "Is that what you really want to do, James?"

He crumples his sandwich bag and sweeps up the crumbs from his desk with his hands. "But you're right," he continues. "If we had the time and made a hundred and fifty pieces a day, it would probably take about one hundred and ten days."

"What if I get the other people to come back?" I ask.

Collins shakes his head and says it's too much work.

"I don't care, I'm gonna try. You give me some paper and I'll start on the new pieces tonight," I insist.

I walk toward the cupboard where he keeps the stacks of colored paper. "I'll make one hundred and fifty by myself tonight, you just wait and see."

"James . . ."

Collins tries to get me to give up, but I won't. All those eyes that are watching me are raising their eyebrows and looking sideways at each other, not sure what I'm gonna do next. Keep it that way.

110

$$150\overline{)16384} = 109.2266$$

150 per Day

Approx 110 Days

22 weeks

approx 5 months

$$5\overline{)110} = 22$$
10
10

$$4\overline{)22} = 5.5$$
20
20
20

$$\begin{array}{r} 150 \\ \times 10 \\ \hline 0 \\ 1500 \end{array}$$

$$\begin{array}{r} 14 \\ +50 \end{array}$$

$$\begin{array}{r} 150 \\ \times 9 \\ \hline 1350 \end{array}$$

Feb March, April, May, June, July
1 2 3 4 5

155

WILLY Q

Don't know what's wrong with kids these days. They're soft. When times are tough, they melt like butter in the hot sun.

A couple of days after talking to my friend Joe at the school, I ask Marcel when he's gonna rebuild that project, and he tells me he's not.

That's what I mean. Soft.

When I was growing up, kids were tougher. Had to be. We were getting married at eighteen or nineteen and getting sent off to war. It wasn't no picnic.

"You just gonna let the people who ruined your project win?" I turn to look at Marcel, who is standing by the counter while I'm shredding some pork for barbecue sandwiches.

Marcel gives me that shrug of his that I don't allow.

I get in his face because I won't stand for that attitude. "You better abandon that rude habit of yours and show me some respect," I warn him, still holding the knife in one hand. "Willy Q's son don't act that way. You disagree with me, you say it to my face. You don't shrug your shoulders at me, you understand?"

Marcel says he does, but I can tell it won't last. I repeat my question. "You gonna let the people who ruined your project win?"

Marcel answers as slow as he can, still being disrespectful, in my opinion.

"Maybe," he says.

He's playing with the coffee stirrers on the counter, making squares and triangles. Doesn't even try to look at me while he's talking.

I give Marcel the list of all the times I could have given up. I count them one by one on my fingers: when my daddy died when I was eight years old, when we lost everything we had in a fire and we had to live in a shelter for three months, when I got drafted, when three of my buddies were killed in Vietnam, when I had to turn my drinking habits around, when the first barbecue place I owned got burnt to the ground and I lost all my money. . . .

"But I never let the enemy win," I say to Marcel. "Death, fire, booze, the Viet Cong, none of them could beat this man" — I point at my chest — "Willy Q. Williams."

"And you ain't gonna give up either," I tell him. "Ain't gonna stand for having no son like that. Williams people don't give up. Your granddaddy didn't give up, I didn't give up, and you ain't going to either." I can feel myself getting emotional, thinking about my own daddy and all, so I try to finish up talking before I do.

"So you just head on back to school tomorrow and start working, all right?" I say, thumping another slab of pork onto the counter. "Whatever time it takes, that's what it takes. I'll look after the Barbecue until you get here. And in between times, you bring me some of that math project because I'm gonna help with making those triangles, too."

I see Marcel's doubting eyes glance at my rough working hands.

"I know they ain't things of beauty, but in the Army, they could sew buttons on a shirt faster than anybody. My buddies called me the Button Man."

Marcel arches his eyebrows. "The Button Man?"

"What? You think all I can do is barbecue?" I give Marcel a smack on the shoulder. "Don't you go doubting the talents of Sergeant Willy Q. Williams."

RHONDELL

My mom says Sharice is someone who has been through a lot. The house on Fifteenth Street wasn't her family's house, it was a foster house. She was being neglected, my mom tells me. I try to imagine what it must feel like to be neglected, how it would feel to live with strangers who didn't care about you.

My mom's anger is fierce when she talks about how Sharice slept on buses and in doorways. "Who would treat a child like that?" she asks. "What kind of world do we live in?"

I wonder why Sharice didn't tell anybody.

My mom says maybe fear, maybe shame, maybe she just didn't know who to tell. "It's not our place to ask questions," my mom warns, "not when we don't know the whole story, not when we haven't walked in her shoes."

The social service agency could have taken Sharice somewhere else, to another temporary place, but Sharice is allowed to stay with us while the agency decides what to do with her. I think this was arranged because of somebody my mom knows at the hospital, even though I don't think it's something my mom wanted to do. I hear her complaining to Aunt Asia, "I take care of people all day, and then I come home and take care of more." With my mom, there are always two sides, the soft side that feels obligated to help everybody and the sharp side that resents always being asked.

Since Sharice is staying with us, I have to loan her some of my clothes, and even a pair of pajamas, because nobody from her old house has cared enough to bring her any clothes. The second night, Aunt Asia drops by with a plastic bag filled with shampoo, conditioner, hair gels, styling creams, toothbrushes, deodorant, combs — things that Sharice doesn't have either.

My mom gives Aunt Asia a disapproving look about some of the things — makeup and nail polish, for instance — but Aunt Asia just laughs at her and says girls will be girls.

Later, I notice how Sharice takes all of Aunt Asia's gifts and arranges them carefully on the little white table next to her bed, as if they are a display in a store. While I'm lying across my bed reading our new book for English, she opens all of the bottles of creams and lotions and oils and tries dabs of each one of them. The whole room starts to smell like grapefruit and oranges and cocoa butter.

"This lipstick tastes just like chocolate chip cookies," she says, smacking her lips together loudly, after trying one of Aunt Asia's lipsticks. "When I lived with my Gram, I remember she used to make the best chocolate chip cookies. . . ." Sharice is quiet for a minute, as if she's waiting for me to say something or look up. "You want to hear about my Gram or are you busy, Rhondell?" she asks softly.

I put down the book I'm holding because this is the first time Sharice has mentioned a word about her family in the two days she's been with us. "If you want to talk about her," I answer carefully. "But you don't have to."

Sharice smiles with her extra-shiny lips. "My Gram was great. . . ." And that night is when the story of her life starts coming out. I don't say much. I just listen.

SHARICE

You ever have the experience of sitting in the comfy stylist's chair at the hair salon, closing your eyes, letting your shoulders down, and just forgetting who you are for a minute?

That's what happens to me on the Friday afternoon that Rhondell's aunt tells us to stop by for a free appointment at the Style R Us salon, where she works. Me and Rhondell both come by after school, even though Rhondell says she'll read magazines and wait, because she doesn't want anything done to her hair.

"Not even a little something?" I try to convince her, but she just shakes her head and tells me her hair is exactly the way she likes it.

It feels strange to walk into the salon and tell them I have an appointment with Asia Taylor. Only a few of the chairs have any customers and they are all moms and grams, with their hair in foil and big plastic clips. (Like some kind of electrical experiment — that's what they look like, you know.) I can feel all of the eyes glancing in the mirrors when I come in. Who's that? the eyes are saying.

Aunt Asia (she says to call her that) keeps stopping and introducing me at each chair as if I am a famous guest. "This is my niece's best friend from school, Sharice Walker." Even though everybody is friendly to me — smiling and shaking my hand, saying how are you, dear — I can see that they can hardly wait to ask a million questions about me later on.

I'd like to be able to tell them it's none of their business that the Sanctuary Baptist Church T-shirt and too-short jeans I'm wearing aren't mine (on loan from Rhondell), or that my appointment is a free gift because I'm poor, or that I'm a foster kid who's had five different non-homes since my Gram died (soon to be six, probably).

But I just smile and act like my friendly old self

and hope Rhondell's aunt won't tell the real story about my whole life after I leave, with all the details that make people pity me. Or if she does, maybe they won't believe a word of it after seeing how happy and confident I looked. (No way that could be true about her, they'll whisper and shake their heads. She looked just like your normal, average girl.)

Once we reach Miss Asia's chair, it feels good to sink into the black leather seat and have the beauty salon cape float down over my head and hide the clothes that aren't mine.

I don't even remember which non-parent took me to the salon, but I think I've only been to one once or twice before. Gram always did my hair herself. She liked to put my hair in braids with those big round beads on the end that look like white gum balls.

Aunt Asia smiles at me in the mirror, and her hand reaches up to smooth one part of her caramel-colored hair, which is arranged in tight little curls all over her head. If Rhondell's mom is plain and simple-looking, Rhondell's aunt is like a fancy frosted cake. Her rows of silver and gold bracelets clank and jangle next to my ear. "Now, I know you are ready to be beautiful,

Miss Sharice," she says, starting to snip the rubber bands out of my hair. "Am I right?"

I nod, thinking how this is probably the only time I'll ever have a chance like this. (Girl, you better savor every minute.) After Aunt Asia finishes conditioning my hair at the sink and brings me back to her chair, I close my eyes and listen to all the voices talking around me. I try to remember the smoky smells drifting from the curling irons and oils and hot combs, and how it feels to sit in the chair like a queen.

While Aunt Asia works on combing out my hair, my mind kinda drifts back a little, and I remember Gram's old hands tugging at my hair when I was little, and how I would sit sideways on one of the chairs in her kitchen, howling and squirming.

You hush now, child, she'd keep on saying. You're gonna wake the dead.

And that always made me wonder, if I screamed loud enough, if my mom would jump up from the grave and come running for me.

I remember doing that once, you know — standing in the middle of Gram's backyard and screaming at the top of my lungs. My poor Gram came flying out the door thinking that I had split open my head, but when she found out why I was screaming, I remember her pulling me against her big chest and saying, Oh honey, the dead are a long, long way away.

And while Rhondell's aunt is tugging at my hair, I start thinking about Gram and my mom and everybody being a long, long way away (and getting farther away), and how Rhondell's aunt is nearby. How she's standing right behind my chair, with her jangling bracelets and her caramel hair, trying to make me look beautiful. How she bought me a shampoo that smelled like sweet grapefruit, and Pink Sunrise nail polish, like my mom or my Gram would have.

And I think I just forget who I am for a minute because I suddenly hear my voice blurting out, "Do you ever think about having somebody stay with you?"

(WHY CAN'T I EVER LEARN TO KEEP MY MOUTH SHUT?)

RHONDELL

About a week after our math club project ends, I see James in the hallway. He's standing by a locker and he turns around quickly when he sees me. "Rhondell," he calls out. "Hey, wait up, I gotta talk to you."

I hug my books tighter and glance around to see who else is in the hallway. I try to pretend I haven't heard anybody call my name. I walk faster, but not so fast that it looks like I am. James catches up. I hear his shoes coming behind me.

"Hey," he says, giving me a hard push. "Hold up."

When I stop walking and look back at him, I'm surprised by what he asks.

He wants to know if I would work on the math project again. "Same group," he says. "You, me, Sharice,

Marcel, Collins, and whoever else shows up. What do you think?" I glance up at his smooth face to see if it's a joke, to see if he's just trying to convince me to answer yes so he can start laughing.

I tell him that I can't work on it. I have other things I have to do at home now.

"What things?" he replies, glaring at me, and I start to wonder if maybe he really means what he's asking, because of how serious he looks.

Just things, I tell him.

What I don't tell him is the real reason I'm saying no. The real reason is that when you have a dream and you see it broken right in front of your eyes, it makes you think that maybe you never should have dreamed it in the first place. It makes you feel like not taking any risks or dreaming any dreams that are too big for yourself again, because you can't tell which ones to trust or what to believe in. And how could anybody say for certain that the people who ruined our first project wouldn't ruin the next one, and the next?

That's what I would like to say to James. Instead I tell him I'm going to be late for class and I can't talk any longer.

But later on, something happens that changes my mind.

In the afternoon, Sharice and I are using the library computer at school. Although we're supposed to be online researching the Romans for history class, Sharice types in the word *tetrahedron* — just to see what appears, she insists.

What comes up is a page about a math professor who studied tetrahedrons years ago. There's a small black-and-white picture of him, wearing thick glasses and a suit and tie, and below the picture, it says his name is Waclaw Sierpinski.

"What kinda name is Waclaw?" Sharice grins, leaning closer to the computer screen. "And how would you say that last name?" She taps her pen on the monitor. "You try saying it first, Rhondell, because you're smarter than me."

But when I try pronouncing it, the name comes out sounding like something a knight in medieval times would be called, Sir Pinski, and Sharice starts getting overcome with laughter, so that even the librarian who is usually nice gives us a sharp look.

Trying not to get us into any more trouble, I duck

my head down behind the monitor to read a little more, and that's where I see the part of the story that changes my mind about working on the tetrahedron again. *Epiphany* would be the college word I'd use for what I find on the page.

Below the picture, the article starts talking about "Sir Pinski" and how he was a math professor from Poland who was known for writing a lot of important math papers and theories. But during World War II, Sir Pinski lost his house and his entire library of mathematical books and research when the Nazis burned them to the ground.

My breath catches in my chest and my eyes blink after I get to those words: "burned to the ground."

All those words and numbers — years and years of work — turned to nothing but ashes? I remember my own college words, only a handful of words, not books and books filled with them. How would it feel to see your own library, a whole lifetime of words and work, lost just like that? In one day?

For the rest of the afternoon, I can't keep my mind from thinking about the mathematician with the name of a knight who saw his library burned to the ground and refused to give up. In a way, the story makes me feel ashamed. We only worked about four months on a simple paper pyramid, just folding paper into triangles, and when the project was ruined, we went our own separate ways and gave up. What if it had been a lifetime of work? A library of words? What then?

That afternoon, I stop by the math classroom and ask Mr. Collins about the possibility of beginning the project again. I tell him I've had a sudden change of mind. An *epiphany*.

AUNT ASIA

"You, raising a kid?"

My sister, Thea, shakes her head.

"You're crazy, Asia. You're just about the least likely foster mom I could imagine," she says. "Think about it. You have to be R-E-S-P-O-N-S-I-B-L-E." (She spells it out.) "You've never been responsible in your entire life, not from day one. I grew up with you, and I know what you're like."

My sister arches her responsible eyebrows and points to herself. "I'm the responsible one," she says. "Working two jobs, raising Rhondell, sending money to half my relatives to keep them on their feet, leading the church choir every Sunday — *that's* responsible."

Both of us reach for another glazed doughnut

from the box in the middle of the table. It's Saturday morning, and Sharice and Rhondell are at the video store getting a movie. The two of us are sitting in the kitchen, drinking coffee and eating doughnuts.

"And what do you know about raising kids, Asia?" my sister continues, taking a bite out of her doughnut. "Rhondell and Sharice are almost high schoolers, and then you've got a whole laundry list of things to worry about," she says. "You gotta watch teenagers, especially girls, like a hawk, you know. You ready to do that?"

I try to tell Thea that she trusts me to help with Rhondell and I've always been there for her. "Name one time I haven't," I say.

My sister counts my other problems on her fingers. "And you've had men trouble, and money trouble, and you don't go to church regular like you should, and you live in a place that doesn't have enough room for a kid, let alone you, and you don't keep your place clean enough for my standards."

She gets up to pour another cup of coffee.

"Don't know why you're even thinking about this, Asia." My sister stands at the counter with the coffeepot in her hand. "You're just being influenced by what that girl told you."

"You didn't hear how she asked if she could stay with me," I argue. "It would have made you cry — I know it would have — the way she asked it."

My sister shakes her head.

I keep on talking.

"And her hair was a mess," I try to explain. "Like nobody had cared about her in years. It was like —" I search for the right words. "It was like her hair was tangled up with all the mess of her life," I say finally. "Like you could almost feel how sad and lonely it must have been for her."

"Sure it was." My sister sits down, still shaking her head. "How do you know that the girl doesn't have mental things wrong with her?" she says, looking at me. "That girl's been in foster care and social services most of her life; think about all the burdens she could be carrying. You ready to deal with all those things?"

"Maybe," I answer, standing up and sticking the box of doughnuts under my arm. "Maybe I am."

MR. COLLINS

A math problem to solve:

If four students and their math teacher begin the tetrahedron project again in February and they work five days a week, making and adding 150 pieces a day to their structure, how many weeks will it take to rebuild the tetrahedron with 16,384 pieces? Extra credit: What if four hairstylists, one Vietnam vet, and a custodian named Mr. Joe also take part?

MARCEL

"Nothing hard about making those little pyramids," Willy Q says, once I show him how you fold the three triangles up to a point, glue the sides together, and hold the sides for about a minute until they stick, and you're done.

Willy Q insists he could do a hundred fifty pieces by himself. One hand tied behind his back. Blind-folded.

When business is slow, me and Willy Q some-times have races at making the pieces. We don't bet money. We bet who has to clean the public bathroom that's outside the Barbecue, or who has to scrub the greasy cooking pans, or who is gonna mop the kitchen floor.

I win, you clean the bathroom. You win, I clean. That's the way we bet.

Or — you win, I wash all the greasy pans. I win, you gotta mop the kitchen floor. On your hands and knees. Twice.

We race making ten at a time. Or twenty. Tetrahedrons go flying across the counter and floor. Willy Q is fast. His fingers don't look fast, but they can move. Sometimes we gotta crawl across the floor and gather up the ones that have flown all over the place.

I win more often than Willy Q. But not much.

Most of the time we have to glue our pieces all over again, or take them apart and refold the sides. "Fast don't always mean good," Willy Q says. "That's a lesson to keep in mind for life — and for working here, too," he adds, giving me a look.

A few days into March we get a warm spell. One of those Pretending-It's-Spring-But-Then-Hit-You-With-a-Blizzard warm spells. Business starts picking up again because people think it's spring even though it isn't. We gotta make tetrahedrons in between ribs and barbecue sandwiches and Singing the Blues wings.

Some people see the bowl of shapes on the

counter and ask, What's that? Some kinda new barbecue sauce packet?

Then Willy Q tells them how they are called tetrahedrons and how my math class is trying to get in the *Guinness Book of World Records*.

For real? they answer, wide-eyed.

Me and Willy Q start handing out pieces for other people to make. Help Washington Middle School get in the records book, Willy Q tells them.

You can always figure out the ones that come from the barbecue. Hold them up to your nose and you can smell the charcoal and wood smoke and barbecue sauce. Better watch your fingers with these, I tell the math club when I bring them in. They're hot, hot, hot.

All the pieces have little Q's written on them, too. "Why you always drawing a little Q on every tetrahedron we make?" I ask Willy Q one afternoon.

He squints at me. "How long you been my son?"

"Thirteen years."

"And all that time, you haven't noticed my name is Willy — Q?"

I grin and pour one of the little sugar packs into my hand. "Stands for Quincy, right?"

185

Willy Q smacks my arm. "Don't you go telling no-body my real name, unless you want to be scrubbing the public toilet with a toothbrush till you're twenty-one — and stop messing with the sugar packs."

"But why put a Q on the tetrahedrons?" I ask.

"Advertising." Willy Q grins. "For the Barbecue. Willy Q. Williams don't do nothing for free."

JAMES HARRIS III

Way back in elementary school, when my brother DJ was in third or fourth grade, he won a basketball jersey signed by four pro players. Half of them don't even play no more, but it's the one thing he's got that means something to him. He always keeps it folded up in a shoebox, taped shut, in the back of the closet underneath a pile of clothes. Nobody's allowed in.

But all rules are off these days with DJ.

One morning, I slip that box out from under the clothes pile, shove it in my backpack, and take it somewhere else. I wait about a week to tell DJ. He's lying on the couch, flipping through channels one night, with a bag of chips sitting on his chest.

"You missing something," I start by saying, and he

flies off the couch like he can read my mind. His hand slams into my chest while he's going past.

"You better not have touched nothing of mine," he swears.

I'm waiting for him when he gets back. "You keep Markese and the others away from our project this time," I tell him.

He gets up in my face. "You gimme that shirt back," he yells.

We keep on repeating the same words over and over, like a CD that's stuck, until my uncle comes slamming out of the bedroom where he was sleeping and tells us both to get out of the apartment, or he's calling the cops.

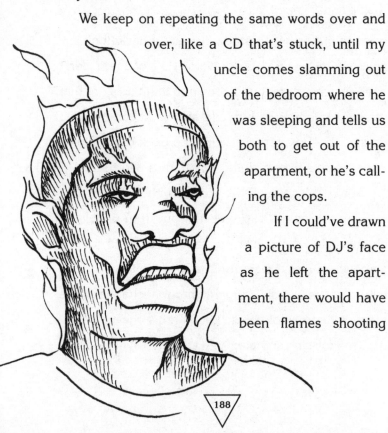

If I could've drawn a picture of DJ's face as he left the apartment, there would have been flames shooting out of his eyes and smoke coming out of his nose and mouth.

But I'm not gonna take any chances this time, not even with my own brother. I lean over the railing of the stairwell and shout that he'll get his jersey back in one piece when the tetrahedron is done. "As long as it stays in one piece — you know what I mean?" I holler. A door slamming is all the answer I get.

SHARICE

I decide it's time to take a chance. I tell Rhondell that she can hand me the yellow or the blue pieces one afternoon when we're working after school, folding and gluing the little tetrahedrons like usual.

Rhondell gives me a quick look. "You sure?" she says. "Because I've got plenty of purple if you want them." She pushes a stack of purple shapes toward me.

"No, I'll take the yellow," I insist. "I'm okay with yellow."

See, I've been trying to change some of the beliefs I have about things (such as the colors blue and yellow). All blue cars don't cause what happened to my mom. For instance, Aunt Asia drives a blue car, and it's about fifteen years old with 174,300 miles and a lot of rust — and nothing has happened to it yet. People are always honking when I'm riding in the car with her because she drives it so slow. You want to scrunch down in your seat sometimes, when people honk their horns and go zooming past, like you're a big blue turtle holding up the whole road.

And when Aunt Asia took me to see her third-floor apartment (at the top of a house) for the first time, to talk about how I might feel about living there, all I could see was yellow when she opened the door. The walls were the yellowest yellow you could imagine. "Isn't that the color of sunshine?" Aunt Asia said, clasping her hands behind her back and happily studying the walls. "That's why I picked it. If I couldn't have an apartment with lots of windows, at least I'd have sunshine, that's what I figured.

"And it won't hurt my feelings if you don't want to stay here after seeing my small place, so don't you worry about that," she told me, twisting her bracelets nervously on her arm and giving me an uncertain look. "It's just me and this little place, and I know it isn't much to offer. Other homes they'd put you in would probably be a whole lot nicer than this."

While she showed me all the things that were wrong with her place — the leaky refrigerator with the towel underneath, and the stove with only one burner that worked, and the rusted bathtub, and the bathroom sink that only ran cold — I thought about how all the things that were wrong with her place were still better than the few things that were right in the other places.

During the tour, I didn't say a word about the yellow walls, either, or tell her how it was my bad luck color. I just said that everything looked fine with me, and I wouldn't mind staying there someday if she didn't mind having me there. (I tried not to sound too hopeful, you know, because hope will get you nowhere.) Aunt Asia gave me a surprised look and said she hadn't made up her mind just yet — that there was still a lot of paperwork to do. . . .

But maybe yellow was my good luck color after all, because Aunt Asia didn't wait very long (like one or two days) before she decided to go ahead with applying to be my foster mom.

And when I thought about those yellow walls later, and how Aunt Asia loved looking at them, I wondered if maybe my Gram was trying to tell me something. Maybe by sending me to a place that was the same color as the flowers I brought to the hospital when she died, she was finally saying thank you to me and telling me it was time to move on.

AUNT ASIA

We talk all the time at the Style R Us hair salon. You know how it is with women. The other stylists are always asking me about Sharice and how she's doing since coming to stay with me at the beginning of May. She into boys yet? they ask. She talk about her past life at all? She adjusting okay to being with you?

I keep a snapshot of her and Rhondell taped in the corner of my mirror. "Those two are my girls," I tell my clients. "That's Miss Rhondell, my sister's girl," I say pointing at Rhondell, who's looking serious in the picture, as usual. "And that's Miss Sharice," I say, pointing at the girl with her hair done up fancy and a wide smile on her face.

I'm not saying we're nosy people at the salon, but

once the other stylists hear how the girls are trying to break a math record with their class at school, they all want to help. Especially after finding out what happened to their first project.

But I have to confess that we have our own sense of style here and we each like to do our own creative things. So after Sharice and Rhondell show us how to make the little pyramids, we can't help giving them a few special touches, like painting them with sparkle nail polish, or giving them purple stripes and gold dots and silver zigzags, or gluing on some rhinestone nail art — just extra little things like that. Sharice says the president of her math club probably won't appreciate our originality. We just laugh and tell her that's all right — most people don't.

My clients are always noticing the pyramids on my counter and asking if they are Christmas tree ornaments. Every time they ask, I have to look at the little piece of paper where Sharice has carefully printed the math word for what they are.

"Tetrahedrons," I explain. "It's something that the kids are studying in math now." Then I bring over

Kyra, our nail tech, and show them how she's painted little gold pyramids on her nails, in honor of the kids.

My clients always shake their heads and say, "Math sure has changed. We never learned words like that when I was in school. Your girl must be real smart, if she's already learning words like that —"

And whenever they talk that way about Sharice, I always feel proud for one quick minute, as if she's my own daughter. And then I remember who I am and I answer, "I don't know where she gets all her math talents from, to tell you the truth. But she's a real hard worker, just like her cousin Rhondell."

Sometimes when Sharice is at school and I'm at home, I slip into her room and look at the photograph of the pretty woman in the lavender dress that she keeps on the little table beside her bed. Sitting there on her bed, I wonder to myself what her mom might have been like and if I'm doing a good job in her eyes.

MR. COLLINS

An important fact to remember about tetrahedrons:

As the tetrahedron structure grows larger and larger, the empty spaces within the tetrahedron grow larger and larger, too.

JAMES HARRIS III

I'm seeing tetrahedrons in my sleep. One thousand eight hundred left to make. The way I figure it, we still got about two more weeks until we're done.

Unless we die of heatstroke first.

"Whose idea was it to sit in a sweaty math room in June working on this project?" I ask. I go over to the windows and point at the neighborhood below us. "Look out there. Everybody else is smart. They're hanging out in the air-conditioning or going to the mall or the movies or wherever. We need some air-conditioning or something in here," I say to Mr. Collins.

Collins is standing on a chair, working on the upper half of the pyramid. He's wearing shorts and a faded green T-shirt that says "Running Man," but you can tell his legs have never run anywhere. They are about as pale and skinny as a chicken's. We started calling him Chicken Legs the first time he wore shorts to math club, and he just smiled and said in the summertime we could call him whatever.

Collins looks around the side of the pyramid. "Air-conditioning?" he repeats, raising his eyebrows. "Maybe you could draw us a big electric fan, James — and then point it in our direction, okay?"

So, I do. Just to make everybody laugh. I go over to the chalkboard and draw a big scary-looking fan with spinning blades. But in the middle of drawing, I notice that the blades I'm sketching are triangles, too. See what I mean? There's no escape. Everything I'm drawing these days is nothing but triangles. Triangle fans. Triangle people. Triangle cars.

Two more weeks . . .

I tell the group that I, for one, don't care if I

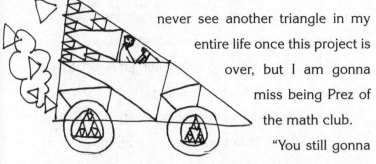

never see another triangle in my entire life once this project is over, but I am gonna miss being Prez of the math club.

"You still gonna call me Prez after this is over?" I ask the group while we're working and sweating. "Because if it wasn't for me, you all woulda quit, I bet. Or you wouldn't have even started on this project again in the first place."

Sharice sends a yellow tetrahedron flying in my direction. "Wasn't for us making nine hundred thousand nine hundred ninety-nine tetrahedrons, you wouldn't have anything to be Prez of," she says.

"Wasn't for me bringing barbecue to eat, you all would have starved," Marcel adds.

Collins tells us if we don't stop wasting time talking and arguing, we're still gonna be here in August. And who wants that?

When he looks away, I whip the tetrahedron piece back at Sharice and hit Rhondell's arm instead. She just glances over her shoulder and gives me the scared-rabbit look she always does. I let out a loud sigh. That girl needs to get more guts or attitude or something.

Maybe because I was spending every day in June at school, gluing little triangles together, that's how I missed what I should have seen coming at my uncle's place. I don't know. I think I was just working so hard on the project at school, trying to be a good Prez and all — eight hours a day some days — that everything at home just went sailing right over my head. Like the tetrahedron flying past Sharice.

But I don't know how I could've missed the big pile of cardboard boxes sitting in the living room of my uncle's apartment, or the official letters stacking up on the kitchen table, or the phone and cable going out and never coming back on.

Or maybe if I noticed those things — why couldn't I have figured out sooner what they meant? Or maybe if, deep down, I knew what they meant, why couldn't it have waited a few more weeks to happen?

MARCEL

Me and Willy Q get a Dog-Days-of-August-and-Everybody-Wants-to-Order-Barbecue customer line in June. Goes all the way out to the parking lot and along the side of somebody's shiny BMW.

"You see that car?" Willy Q hollers from the grill. "We are hot, hot, hot tonight."

Me, I'm wearing my special Sorry-You-Had-to-Wait-For-an-Hour-But-That's-the-Way-It-Goes smile. Taking orders as fast as my hand can write.

"What can I get for you tonight, sir?"

"How can I help you, ma'am?"

"We got Blast Off to Outer Space Hot, Melt the Roof of Your Mouth Hot, Wait in Line for Ten Years Hot. . . ."

One whole family of white folks wants everything

mild. Why'd you come to a barbecue in the first place? I want to ask. Why not just sit at home and eat plain bread and water?

"You got fried green tomatoes?" one old hunchbacked black lady with a Southern accent asks me.

"Nope."

"Black-eyed peas?"

"Nope."

"Why'd I wait forever in this line, then, young man?"

A black man in a fine-looking suit and red tie asks me, "What's Tar in the Summertime Hot? And how's that different than Plain Ol' Hot?"

I lean on the counter and give him one of my You-Better-Not-Ask-Me-Any-More-Questions-Because-There-Are-Fifty-People-Behind-You-In-Line-or-Haven't-You-Noticed smiles. "One's hotter than the other," I tell him.

It's almost dark when James comes up to the window. Turn back to the counter to take another order and see him standing there. Moths and bugs flitting around his head like halos. "Hey," I say, forgetting all my customer speeches. "How's it going, Prez?" Reach my hand through the order window so he can smack it.

Willy Q looks over from the grill. "We got lots of people still waiting," he says. "Ain't time for socializing with your friends, Marcel. Ask him to come back later."

"He's ordering," I call out to Willy Q. Then I tell the Prez that I'll give him Marcel's special No-Charge Discount. Ask Willy Q to fix up two Singing the Blues, a side of cornbread, and one homemade lemonade for him.

James slips an envelope through the window. "Give this to Collins tomorrow," he says. "It's a note for him."

"Why can't you?" I ask.

"Things to do," he answers.

I slip the Prez's food out through the window. Two boxes of wings, one bag of cornbread, and a cup of cold lemonade with lotsa ice rattling in the cup. "That'll be twelve fifty-seven, thank you very much," I say loudly, opening and closing the window like he's just paid me for the food.

"You crazy, Marcel," the Prez says, grinning.

Willy Q shouts behind me, "Get busy, Marcel."

"Don't forget to give Collins that letter," the Prez finishes, talking fast. "And make sure he does what it says." He points at me. "I'm counting on you, Marcel." And then he slips away into the darkness.

I only remember that last part later. Me and Willy Q are cleaning up the place, and suddenly Marcel the Magnificent's mind stops and thinks — what's he counting on me for?

MR. COLLINS

Dear Mr. Collins,

It's Friday night and I'm writing you this letter to tell you and everybody that I won't be back at math club. My uncle is moving tonight and he doesn't know where but I won't be there when the tetrahedron is finished and I did a lot of work on it, but everything isn't easy is it? I wrote out some things for everybody to do and they better do them right.

Here they are:

1. Don't forget the top part should be almost all red with a few orange. Don't make any more blue, green, or purple ones - there's enough already!

2. Make sure that everything is glued right, especially at the top.

3. Don't forget my name when you're talking to the Guinness World Records people. I want it spelled James Harris III ok? (Don't forget the III.)

4. Mr. Collins – remember to call the newspapers and TVs and maybe the National Enquirer, too.

5. DON'T GIVE UP!!!!!

6. Marcel – you can be the Prez now instead of me as long as you don't mess up.

I would work on the tetrahedron some more if I could but I'm proud of it anyway. Remember everyone – DON'T GIVE UP (or I'll kick your butt)!!!!!

Bye for now,

James Harris III

P.S. It was fun while it lasted

RHONDELL

Nobody says a word after Mr. Collins finishes reading the letter to us. I can hear the smack of a basketball on the street outside and the sound of locusts whirring in the trees and a car alarm going off somewhere, but inside the math room, the four of us are silent.

"Are you sure this letter came from him?" Mr. Collins asks Marcel.

Marcel nods.

Sharice leans forward. "Did he look sad or upset or anything?"

Marcel shrugs his shoulders and keeps his eyes on the floor. "Not that I saw."

I can hear Mr. Collins sigh as he's folding up the letter. He leaves it sitting on his chair as he stands up and walks over to the open windows that face the streets. His hands are in his pockets, and his head shakes back and forth. I know he's seeing a whole neighborhood of run-down, poor houses with people like James' family, who never stick around, but I want to tell him that's not true of everybody. My mother's family has always lived in the neighborhood, and Marcel's father has, too. My grandma sang in the Sanctuary Baptist Church Choir when she was a girl, and one of my uncles helped to build the gymnasium of Washington Middle School years ago. *Permanence* is the college word for us.

Sharice reaches for the letter on Mr. Collins' chair. "Didn't he leave an address or phone number or anything?" she says, unfolding the letter to read it again. But I guess there isn't anything else written there because Sharice quietly puts the letter back where it was.

I don't know how I feel about James leaving. How should I feel? I wonder.

I look over at the big tetrahedron and see all the colors he made us assemble by following the exact order of a rainbow. It looks beautiful, that's a fact. Next to the tetrahedron is a big poster he was starting to color with Magic Marker. It says "THE RAINBOW TETRAHEDRON PROJECT."

But I remember the first day of math club, too, when he was sitting in the corner of the room with his sweatshirt pulled over his head, spinning quarters on his desktop. I remember how he always called my name Ron Dull, no matter how many times Sharice and Mr. Collins told him to stop it.

In a way, he was like the tetrahedrons we made, I think to myself. He started out being just a plain old flat sheet of paper — angry and mean paper, most of the time. And then, slowly, he began to turn into someone else, with different sides and angles to who he was, and some of those sides were okay. He was a talented artist and mostly a good Prez, but other parts stayed the same —

Marcel smacks his hands together, making all of us jump out of our sad thoughts. "Why you sitting here doing nothing?" he says, trying to copy James' tough expression and voice. "We got a hundred and fifty pieces to do today. That's the rule. Get up and get busy, girl." He pretends to tug on Sharice's reluctant arm. "I'm the new Prez now and you better do what I sez."

That gets all of us laughing. Even Mr. Collins turns away from the window, smiling a little. Although we can't stand looking at the blinding color red all day, we make one hundred and eighty-one red pieces, a new record. The Prez would be proud of us, Marcel says.

SHARICE

As we get closer to finishing, I start having dreams about what's gonna happen when we do. In most of my dreams, there is this big flash of light when we finish the tetrahedron, and our school isn't a crumbling, peeling-paint building anymore. It's rainbow-colored. (I know this sounds kinda weird.) And our giant pyramid sits on top of the school roof shooting out colors all over the neighborhood, like spotlights. Houses turn shades of red and orange and blue. And people stop their cars and roll down their windows, to take pictures of the sight.

Rhondell just shakes her head when I tell her about my dreams. We're walking home from math club, eating chocolate ice-cream cones from the Super Scoop Ice Cream Shop. It must be about 100 degrees.

"I don't think it will be anything like that," she says.

"How do you know? Nobody's ever finished one before."

Rhondell rolls her eyes. "Sharice . . ."

But it was true — when we put the last piece on the top, none of us knew what would happen after that.

MARCEL

Hope nobody wants a Melt the Roof of Your Mouth barbecue sandwich on Monday at noon, because Willy Q's Open-Every-Day-of-the-Year-Except-Christmas Barbecue is closed. Willy Q says he wouldn't miss the tetrahedron celebration for all the customers in the world.

"You kidding?" I ask him when he tells me on Sunday that he's closing the grill.

"You think I'm lying, Marcel?" He gives me one of his Army stares. Then, a smile splits across his face and he drapes his arm across my shoulders.

"You didn't let the name Williams down and I'm real proud of you for that," he says, squeezing my shoulders hard. "I thought maybe you would, but you didn't, and so we're gonna celebrate the first Williams in the *Guinness Book of World Records*. Who woulda thought it'd be in math?"

"And now" — he snaps his fingers — "do I have a surprise for you. Wait there. Watch the ribs on the top rack."

While I'm keeping an eye on the ribs, he wipes his hands on his apron and goes into the back room. Comes out holding a new suit and tie. Shiny dark gray suit with a metallic silver tie.

"Man, that is sharp," I say. "That for me?"

Willy Q nods. "Cost me a mint."

"It's like being in the Academy Awards or something."

Willy Q laughs. "Not much different," he says.

Then he goes in the back room again. Comes out holding a black T-shirt with the words "Willy Q's BBQ, Cleveland, Ohio" on the front in huge white letters. Phone number just below the name. "This is what I'm wearing," he says. "What do you think?" He squints at the shirt. "Will folks on national TV be able to read our phone number?"

You just gotta admire Willy Q sometimes.

"One more thing I've been working on," he says, going over to one of the metal warming pans. He picks up a barbecue wing, puts it on a paper plate, and brings it over to me. "Try this new sauce."

I pick up the wing with the end of my fingers. Try to cool it off by blowing on it.

"Stop being a baby," Willy Q says. "Just eat it."

The sauce is sweet and kinda spicy, too. Willy Q points to a pan on the counter. "That's my new sauce. Guess what it's called?"

I give up after about ten guesses.

Willy Q smacks his hands together. "Willy Q's Tangy Tetrahedron Barbecue Sauce. A little brown sugar, a little lemon juice, some ketchup, some green celery — you know, a sauce with some *color* to it —

"And of course," he adds with a grin, "a few secret ingredients we won't tell nobody. Because in barbecue you always gotta have a secret or two."

Tangy Tetrahedron Barbecue Sauce

2 tablespoons butter or margarine

3 tablespoons chopped onion

½ cup chopped green celery

2 tablespoons brown sugar

1 tablespoon Worcestershire sauce

2 tablespoons malt vinegar

¼ cup lemon juice

1 teaspoon dry mustard

1 cup red ketchup

Melt butter in a small skillet. Sauté onions and celery in butter until tender. Combine remaining ingredients in a saucepan. Add sautéed onions and celery from the skillet, and bring sauce to a boil. Simmer over low heat for about 10 to 15 minutes, stirring to blend the sweet and tangy colors and flavors.

MR. COLLINS

A few last facts you should know:

1. The tetrahedron project was completed at the end of the first week in July.

2. It took about twenty-one weeks, more than three thousand sheets of paper, and hundreds of glue sticks to finish.

3. The final tetrahedron was close to nine feet tall with 16,383 pieces.

4. The students at Washington Middle School beat
   the California record by 12,287 pieces — or
   more if you include the first tetrahedron.

5. But one piece was still missing. . . .

SHARICE

Early on Monday morning (and I mean early), we meet at the school. I think all of us are kinda nervous, you know. Mr. Collins says the media's coming at noon. We stand on the front steps of the school rubbing our goose-bumpy arms, even though it's July and it isn't even cold. As Mr. Collins unlocks the door, Marcel tries to make everybody crack up by saying we're way too early for school in September, but nobody laughs.

We walk down the empty hallway and up the steps, with our shoes echoing loudly on the tiles. To tell you the truth, we look like we're going to church, the way we're all dressed up. Marcel and Mr. Collins are wearing suits. (Marcel looks kinda good, but you didn't hear that from me.) I've got a red skirt and a new blouse that Aunt Asia just bought for me, and I'm wearing a pair of her nice red shoes with Kleenex stuffed in the toes to make them fit.

Me and Aunt Asia even talked Rhondell into doing a little something with her hair, so it is pulled back with a nice puff of curls. She's wearing one of her church dresses, but her mom said no earrings or lipstick. Her mom is strict.

When we get up to the third floor where the math room is, we see the shadow of something near the math room door at the other end of the dark hall. I don't know about anybody else, but my heart starts to thump in my chest, because I remember what happened before (don't even think about it, girl . . .).

But as we get closer, I can see that the shadow is a person sitting in a folding chair next to the door. The person is Mr. Joe, the custodian.

He has a plaid blanket across his lap, and beside him is a classroom desk with a clock, a silver thermos, and a little radio on the top. A baseball bat is leaning against the other side of the desk, I notice, too.

"Have you been here all night?" Mr. Collins asks in a surprised voice.

"Yes sir," Mr. Joe says. He gestures with his thumb at the closed door behind him. "Just makng sure nobody was getting in again. No way." He points to the baseball bat and grins. "Not if I had anything to say about it."

Standing up slowly, the custodian starts folding up the blanket and packing up his things. "Wish I could stay for all the news and pub-licity. I hear there's gonna be a lot," he tells us. "But I'm not much for all that, and I need something to eat, that's what I need. And a bed." He turns to give us one last look before he shuffles down the steps. "You all sure do look nice, though," he says, holding on to the railing and looking back up. "Like grown-ups overnight."

After the custodian leaves, Mr. Collins unlocks the door to the math room and opens it. We don't even turn on the lights at first. We just take in the sight of that huge pyramid shimmering in the dusty morning sunlight coming through the old windows. In the shadowy room, the colors look like they're glowing — purples and blues and greens — as if they aren't paper anymore, but something else. (Not spotlights, but close.)

We walk around the tetrahedron, trying to see it from different angles. The top almost touches the ceiling tiles. With all of the open spaces letting in the light, the triangle pieces look as if they're floating in the air. Glancing through the open spaces, you can see parts of the room and flickers of sunlight and other people's blinking eyes looking back at you.

Nobody says a word for a while because all we want to do is walk around and admire our work, I guess. I get the feeling that everybody is seeing something different, though, as they're walking around. Me, I'm seeing that very first day when I decided to come to the club to get out of sitting in the blue plastic library chairs. (Wasn't my life sure a mess then?) I see James sitting in the corner, and Mr. Collins not having a clue about what he was doing, and Rhondell with her nose in a book not even knowing that she would become my half-cousin, or foster cousin, or whatever it is we are now.

Mr. Collins flips on the overhead lights, making us all squint. "Time to get ready," he says, "before the guests arrive."

RHONDELL

The math room is filled, wall-to-wall, with people. My mom is there, and Aunt Asia is standing in the front with the beauty-shop ladies on their lunch break, and the pastor of the Sanctuary Baptist Church is somewhere in the crowd. Marcel said his daddy even closed the barbecue, just so he could come.

It is hot, even with the windows wide open and bees buzzing in. As I walk up to the front to stand next to the tetrahedron, my heart is pounding and my legs feel like they are trembling enough for everybody to be able to notice them.

Take a deep breath, Rhondell, I hear my mom whispering inside my head. Pretend you are in church, standing up to sing with the choir.

I'm giving the part of the presentation about the math facts we learned. I hear my voice explaining about tetrahedrons and telling the story of Waclaw Sierpinski and what happened to his library. My voice is shaky at first and I keep looking down at the notes on my paper, but then the college words that I've been saving for years start pouring out. *Epiphany. Metamorphosis. Estimation. Determined* . . .

I see Mr. Collins nodding and nodding, so I know I'm doing all right, and I don't look in the direction of the TV cameras at all. I just keep my eyes on the math club and think about those college doors swinging open to let Rhondell Jeffries inside. When I finish, everybody claps and Mr. Collins says, "You can see why we think this young lady is one of our best and brightest," and everybody claps again.

One of the reporters asks us if we had any favorite colors when we were working on the project. The three of us — Mr. Collins, Marcel, and I — look in the direction of Sharice. She waves her hand in the air and says, "Okay, okay, I'm the one who kinda liked purple."

A woman reporter with blond hair and silver

glasses asks us why we decided to participate in the project in the first place. We look at each other, trying to decide who will reply first, and I'm surprised when my voice answers before anybody else and tells the reporter that I hope to go to college someday, and that's why I joined the math club.

"What particular college would you like to attend?" the reporter wants to know, and my heart begins pounding in my chest. Everybody stares at me, waiting for an answer, and I realize that I never saw a name printed on those college doors in my mind. They were just fancy wooden doors with iron hinges and ivy plants trailing along the sides.

"She's planning on going to Harvard," my Aunt Asia calls out in the silence. "Right, Rhondell?" And I can see my mom give her a poke with her elbow to hush up.

"Harvard — or wherever it wouldn't cost too much," I answer quickly, and everybody laughs.

After that, Mr. Collins and Marcel pull a stepladder over to the tetrahedron to add the final piece at the very top, for the cameras. The room is as silent as a church prayer. With the afternoon sun coming through the windows and Marcel standing on the top of the ladder in his fancy gray suit and silver tie, I have to admit that he looks almost like a movie star.

"I don't know how his daddy afforded to buy a suit like that," Sharice whispers to me.

I can see Marcel's father standing near the doorway of the classroom looking proud, as all of the cameras get ready to show Marcel putting the last red tetrahedron on the top. Mr. Collins helps him add the glue to the piece, he reaches toward the top, and then his hand freezes in midair.

"Just a minute," he says, relaxing his arm and giving his movie-star smile for all the cameras. "I'm not quite ready."

After a minute or so, he raises his arm again, turns to smile at the cameras, and puts the last tetrahedron, number 16,384, at the top. "This one's for James Harris III," he says, and all the cameras flash like spotlights.

JAMES HARRIS III

What's taking them so long? Every day for two weeks, I walk down to the convenience store on the corner, buy a paper, open it up, and look for a picture, and then feel like a fool when nothing is there.

"You looking for somebody you know?" the old store manager asks me.

"Some friends," I tell him, and each day, he waits until I page through the whole paper piece by piece, even the sports section, before he says, "Not there today?"

"Nope."

"Maybe tomorrow," he always answers, and then he pushes a peppermint candy or a piece of chocolate or something across the counter toward me.

"Here — consolation prize," he says, and after two weeks, I get the feeling that he's starting to think I'm just coming in the store for the consolation prize. When I walk through the door, I can see his head shake back and forth a little.

"You know," he tells me one evening when I stop by, "I've heard that getting in the newspaper isn't all that easy. Too much news to cover these days, and so the reporters have to pick and choose. . . ."

I tell him that they'll be in the paper.

The old man's head shakes back and forth again.

And then, one Tuesday night, I open up the newspaper and there it is.

"No way," I say out loud, and the old man slams the cash drawer shut and comes hurrying over from behind the counter to see what I'm looking at. He pulls a paper off the stack and turns to the same page I'm on.

A photograph fills almost half the page. Page 4A. "Students Break Math Record!" the headline says. The photo shows Marcel, who doesn't even look like Marcel, wearing a sharp-looking suit and tie like he's a big star or something. He's standing on a ladder, grinning like a fool, as he's getting ready to put the last tetrahedron on the top.

I squint at the picture, trying to tell if the tetrahedron is red or not. Better be red, Marcel. At the side of the picture, Mr. Collins and Rhondell and Sharice are standing there, watching. Only person missing is me.

But then I see the first sentence at the beginning of the article: "'This one's for James,' seventh grader Marcel Williams says, as he proudly puts the final touches on the 16,384-piece tetrahedron built by a group of inner-city kids in Cleveland, Ohio."

"I'm the James he's talking about here," I tell the store manager. "Look at that first sentence." I point at the words. "That's me."

The store manager's eyes go from the newspaper to me and back again. "You're a math champion?" he asks, like he doesn't quite believe I'm telling the truth.

"That's right." I nod. "My name is gonna be in the *Guinness Book of World Records* someday."

The old man sticks out his hand. "Well, let me shake your hand, son," he says in a formal voice. "I've never met anybody who had a world record before."

And then he lays the paper on the store counter and carefully cuts out the article and the photograph. "This is a real accomplishment," he says while he's cutting. "You should be real proud of yourself." He asks me to put my autograph on the article so when I'm famous someday, he can show people my name and say he met me in his store.

I sign my name across the bottom of the article in big scrawling artist letters. But before the manager tapes the article to the front of the counter where everybody can see it, I add one more thing.

I add a drawing of myself standing next to Sharice and Rhondell and Mr. Collins, with an arrow pointing to my head. I write my name above the arrow: James Harris III.

Just so everybody knows I was there.

MR. COLLINS

One final fact to remember about tetrahedrons:

Because of its repeating pattern, the tetrahedron structure can expand to infinity. So, in theory, you can keep
adding more and more tetrahedrons forever. . . .

Our math teacher Mr. Collins says that next year Washington Middle School is gonna build something even bigger, something even more amazing.

So if you are driving down Washington Boulevard someday, past the smoky good smells of Willy Q's Barbecue, past the Style R Us hair salon where they do nails like nobody's business, past the eye-popping red doors of the Sanctuary Baptist Church, and you get to a dead end — LOOK UP!

You just might see a forty-foot-tall silver and gold tetrahedron on the roof of our school building spinning to rap music.

Mr. Collins says nothing is impossible.

You want to fold silver or gold?

AUTHOR'S NOTE

This book began with a visit to an inner-city middle school in Cleveland, Ohio, where I discovered something spectacular: a 16,384-piece rainbow-colored pyramid that was over eight feet tall! The project captured my imagination. Immediately I wanted to know more about the school and its students—and about the record-breaking creation.

The name of the school was Alexander Hamilton Middle School, although I renamed it "Washington Middle School" in the book. The school was indeed

Former Alexander Hamilton Middle School, Cleveland, Ohio

a place of broken windows and peeling paint when I saw it. The building itself was more than seventy years old, and the neighborhood around it was old and crumbling, too. Many families in the area struggled with poverty and a lack of opportunities.

However, in 2002, a group of students and teachers at the school decided to build something big— something no other school had successfully completed. They wanted to build a "Stage 7" Sierpinski tetrahedron. They named it "The Rainbow Connection" because of the eye-catching and intricate rainbow pattern they created.

Original Stage 7 rainbow tetrahedron, 2002

SO...HOW DID THEY DO IT?

During the original project, the team used an Ellison die-cutting machine to stamp out the tiny tetrahedron shapes, which were not much bigger than postage stamps. The machine saved one step in the laborious process, but each one of the 16,384 shapes still had to be individually folded, glued, and joined together—just as the characters describe. Hot-glue guns, used for model-building and craft projects, proved to be the best tool for joining the pieces and sections together. The students worked at home, during school, and after school to finish the structure. They estimated that it took about five months to complete.

During the writing of *All of the Above*, I read everything I could find about tetrahedrons—and also polished up some of my long-dormant math skills. I was often amazed by the connections between math and life. Mr. Collins' facts about tetrahedrons are based on the actual properties of the structure—and yes, a tetrahedron really can be expanded to infinity. But I'm not planning to try that anytime soon!

One mathematical note from the fictional Mr. Collins: Although some of the characters in the story used the terms "pyramid" and "tetrahedron" interchangeably, keep in mind that a tetrahedron is a special type of pyramid with a triangular base. Other types of pyramids with bases of different shapes would not be tetrahedrons.

Professor Waclaw Sierpinski, who is mentioned in the novel, is the person who first studied the properties of the tetrahedron as a flat, plane figure called a "gasket." As Rhondell learns, he was a renowned math professor in Warsaw, Poland, during the early part of the twentieth century. Even though his house and personal library were destroyed by the Nazis during the Warsaw uprising of 1944, he went on to publish more than seven hundred research papers and fifty books in his lifetime.

While many of the characters and events in the novel are fictional, I tried to capture the spirit and determination of the real team. Like the characters in the story, they did have favorite colors and tasks, and working on the project did bring them closer together as a group. I also wanted to give readers a glimpse into the challenges faced by kids growing up in poverty, who, like Sharice and James, sometimes struggle with problems like homelessness and hunger.

During the research for the book, I spent time observing the math team and interviewing the team leaders at Alexander Hamilton Middle School. At the time, the students were already hard at work on a new construction— an inverted Stage 6 tetrahedron. It was designed to match the colors of the Ohio flag and to spin to music.

Stage 6 inverted tetrahedron, 2003

I'm often asked if the school ever got an official Guinness World Record.

While the team attempted to submit their record to Guinness World Records for consideration, the process was never fully completed. However, the team and their teachers believe their Stage 7 tetrahedron did set a record as the first one ever built—an achievement by itself.

In 2006, Alexander Hamilton Middle School closed its well-worn doors forever, and the school was eventually torn down. However, during the last decade, many schools have been inspired by the story to create their own tetrahedrons. The popularity of STEM (Science, Technology, Engineering, and Math) programs has increased the interest in all aspects of math and technology. Tetrahedrons can be found in chemistry, engineering, art, architecture, and design.

In recent years, several schools across the country have tackled and met the challenge of a Stage 7. Many more have made Stage 6 tetrahedrons. Some have designed and flown tetrahedral kites. I hope that the novel inspires you to set your own world record or to create something spectacular—maybe the first-ever Stage 8?

And always remember...nothing is impossible!

—*Shelley Pearsall*

Stage 5 tetrahedron

OTHER RESOURCES

Visit Shelley Pearsall's websites to find more activities for the book: www.onebookoneday.com and www.shelleypearsall.com.

Learn more about tetrahedrons and build a tetrahedral kite at: www.illuminations.nctm.org (Keyword: tetrahedrons).

To purchase Ellison tetrahedron dies: www.ellison-education.com.

ACKNOWLEDGMENTS

I would like to thank editors Jennifer Hunt and Alvina Ling and assistant editor Nikki Garcia, who helped to bring this story to life (twice!), and illustrator Javaka Steptoe who stepped into the shoes of James Harris III to create the artwork for the book. A tetrahedron-sized thank-you to the 2002–2003 math teams at Alexander Hamilton Middle School, their teachers James Wallace and Dianne Marsh, and Principal Hiawatha Shivers. I'm indebted to math teachers Laura and Richard Little for answering my math questions, as well as local students Cameron Granger and Artia Gunn, who read my early drafts. And finally, I can't forget to mention my family—without their culinary advice and assistance in preparing (and tasting!) the recipes for the book, Willy Q and I would both be singing the blues.

HOW TO BUILD A TETRAHEDRON

A tetrahedron is a type of pyramid, made up of four triangles of equal size. Make a copy of this tetrahedron model. Color it, cut it out, and tape it together to make your own tetrahedron.

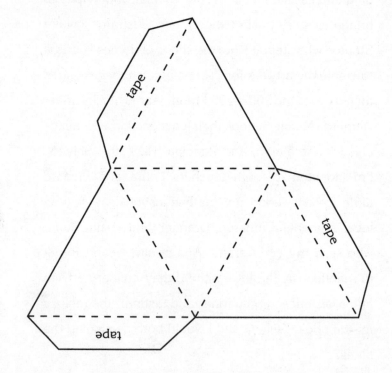

Next, tape your tetrahedrons together in sets of four to form larger tetrahedrons. These can be combined to form even larger tetrahedrons, if desired.

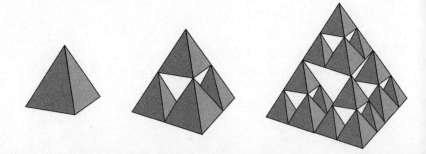

READER'S GUIDE

1. James Harris III dislikes school and anything connected with it. How does James's home life affect his attitude toward school? How does Mr. Collins's approach to James pull him into the project? How does James's attitude toward himself change as he becomes involved in the project? How do others' opinions of James change?

2. Although Mr. Collins has the idea for the tetrahedron project, he doesn't really expect that any of his students will want to participate (page 18). What is the motivation for each of the students to become involved in the project? How does Mr. Collins's lack of expertise in running a club help unite the students to work toward a common goal?

3. James and Sharice both feel responsible for the destruction of the project. How does that guilt affect them? What actions do they take as a result of their feelings of responsibility? How do their guilt and shame affect the group and the completion of the project?

4. What contributions, both positive and negative, do the adults make in the lives of James, Rhondell, Marcel, and Sharice? How do the actions of the adults affect the lives of the teens?

5. Rhondell and her aunt Asia are the ones who find Sharice after her emotional breakdown. How does this one event alter the course of many lives?

6. The author reveals that the role of each of the four students in the group mirror a tetrahedron in some way. Discuss the role each character plays in the group. How do each character's personality traits determine how he or she is like a tetrahedron? Reread Mr. Collins's words about tetrahedrons on pages 3, 99, 199, and 237 to gain some insight.

7. In the end, how does the project change Rhondell, Marcel, James, Sharice, and Mr. Collins? Predict what the future may hold for these characters.